THE MYSTERY O

Gothic Classics

MYSTERY OF THE BLACK TOWER

by

John Palmer, Jun.

Edited and with an introduction by James D. Jenkins

VALANCOURT BOOKS

CHICAGO

The Mystery of the Black Tower
ISBN 0-9766048-1-7
Library of Congress Control Number: 2005920881

Published by Valancourt Books, Chicago, Illinois

Originally published in 1796
First Valancourt Books edition August 2005

Cover photograph by Ryan Cagle

Printed in the United States of America

CONTENTS

Introduction by James D. Jenkins   vii

Note on the Text   xiv

Author's Dedication   1

The Mystery of the Black Tower by John Palmer   3

Appendix:

    List of subscribers to the first edition (1796)   179

    Review of the novel from the *British Critic* (1797)   184

INTRODUCTION

There seems still to persist, even today, a great deal of unnecessary confusion about the author of *The Mystery of the Black Tower*. The novel has often been wrongly attributed, and indeed still is, in a number of library catalogues, to John Palmer of Bath, a literary schoolmaster who published works of poetry. Montague Summers, in his *The Gothic Quest*, long ago refuted this contention, and the reason why it persists is an enigma. When the novel was translated into French in 1799, it was attributed to "Jh. Palmer, le célèbre acteur de Londres." John Palmer was, in fact, a celebrated actor of the time, but it was not he, but his son, John Palmer, Jun. (1771-1810), who wrote *The Mystery of the Black Tower*.

The younger Palmer seems to have led a very difficult life. He was the eldest of eight children, and despite his father's great renown as one of the premier actors of his day, the family always lived on the verge of poverty. Palmer's mother died at an early age, and his father, greatly distressed at her death, famously died in 1798 while performing the third act of Kotzebue's *The Stranger*. He spoke the lines "Oh, God! oh, God!/There is another and a better world!" then fell to the ground. The audience, supposing his fainting fit to be part of the play, applauded loudly, before the truth was announced, that Palmer had really died.

The younger Palmer followed in his father's footsteps, making his first appearance in 1791 at the Haymarket as Prince Hal to his father's Falstaff. He turned to writing novels in 1795, not for the same reason as some Gothic novelists, such as Horace Walpole, M.G. Lewis, Ann Radcliffe, or even Francis Lathom, who wrote for amusement and to express their creativity, but rather to provide for himself and his family.

His first novel, *The Haunted Cavern: a Caledonian Tale,* was published in 1795, a year after Radcliffe's *Mysteries of Udolpho* and a year before Lewis's *The Monk*. As Allen Grove writes in his introduction to *The Cavern of Death* (also available in Valancourt's *Gothic Classics* series), caverns, caves, and grottos were extremely

common settings for Gothic novels in the last years of the eight-
eenth century and the first few years of the nineteenth. Palmer,
recognizing the market for such a work, penned *The Haunted
Cavern,* liberally borrowing from these earlier "Grotto Gothics," as
Professor Frank terms them. He appropriated a number of plot
devices from *The Cavern of Death* (1794), including, notably, the
haunted cavern which contains the body of the hero's murdered
father. *The Critical Review* for December 1795 deplored *The
Haunted Cavern'*s lack of originality, writing that "the tale of
shrieking spectres, and bloody murders, has been repeated till it
palls upon the sense." But the reviewer's disdain did nothing to
dampen the immense popularity of the book, which was reprinted
at Dublin, New York, and Baltimore in 1796, and remained in
print until at least 1814.

Only a year after his first novel, Palmer published his second,
The Mystery of the Black Tower. One very interesting aspect of
this novel's publication can be found on its title page, which reads
"Printed for the author by William Lane at the Minerva Press."
William Lane's Minerva Press was the great purveyor of Gothic
fiction between 1790 and 1820, churning out dozens of titles per
year to satisfy the seemingly inexhaustible demand for Gothic
fiction by the reading public. Generally Lane purchased the copyright from the author, then was free to print as many editions as he
liked of the book, reaping all the profits. *Mystery of the Black
Tower,* by contrast, was published by subscription, which is to say
that Palmer secured the pledges of a large number of individuals to
purchase his book upon its publication, and he financed the print-
ing himself.[1] It is unclear what Palmer's motive was for publishing

---

[1] One scholar's recent work indicates just how unusual it was that Lane
printed *Mystery of the Black Tower* for its author. In Deborah Anne McLeod's
dissertation *The Minerva Press* (University of Alberta, 1997), she examines
1,636 works printed by Lane and his successor A.K. Newman, from 1777-
1838. Of these works, twenty or fewer were printed by Lane and Newman for
the authors, and of this handful, only a few were novels, mostly long-
forgotten works like *The Shrine of Bertha* (1794) and *Memoirs of the Princess
of Zell* (1796). The only other significant work printed for its author at the
Minerva Press was Richard Sickelmore's Gothic shocker *Mary-Jane* (1800).

by subscription, rather than simply selling the rights to the novel to Lane or another publisher. Subscription was fraught with difficulties, as P. D. Garside points out in his article *Subscribing Fiction in Britain, 1780-1829.* The author frequently faced humiliation by soliciting subscriptions, as it had the appearance (if not the reality) of seeking charity. And, as Garside notes, subscribers were frequently quicker to sign up than to pay.

Subscription was most often used by previously unknown writers, who were not able to attract the attention of a publisher, and who wanted to get their work out in the public eye. However, Palmer was not a novice writer; his previous novel had been a huge success. Presumably a publisher would have felt fortunate to purchase the manuscript to *Mystery of the Black Tower*, which, like its predecessor, went on to be quite successful.

So, why then did Palmer decide to publish it by subscription? Perhaps after selling the manuscript of *The Haunted Cavern* for a trifling sum, then watching it go on to become an international bestseller, Palmer thought he could make more money by retaining the copyright and publishing the book himself. Whatever Palmer's reasons for publishing the novel as he did, *Mystery of the Black Tower* was successful (if less so than *The Haunted Cavern*), running through another edition, published at York in 1802, and being translated into French and printed at Paris in 1799 and 1821.

Curiously, Palmer followed the success of his two Gothic romances with a more serious novel, *The World as it Goes; or, Portraits from Nature* (1803), which was apparently not very well-received, and, indeed, remains utterly forgotten today. He followed that effort with a book more suited to his talents, *The Mystic Sepulchre; or, Such Things Have Been* (1806), a fine Gothic romance, which, while just as formulaic as his other Gothic novels, proved just as enjoyable and just as popular. It was translated into French in 1810, the year before Palmer's death, as *Le Tombeau mystérieux, ou les Familles de Hénarez et d'Almanza.*

Palmer's final work, *Like Master, Like Man*, was published posthumously in 1811, a year after his death at age 39, bearing the sad inscription "Printed for the Relief of the Author's Widow" on its title page, and containing a preface by the playwright George Colman, the Younger.

Scholars of Gothic fiction generally divide the novels of the period into two "schools": the more lyrical and subdued romances of Ann Radcliffe and her followers, which sought to evoke "sublime" terror, and the novels of the so-called German, or *schauerromantik* writers, such as M. G. Lewis, whose *The Monk* (1796) inspired horror through an accumulation of shocking and gruesome events. But there was also a third major subset of Gothic novels, which looked back further than Radcliffe or Lewis's novels for inspiration: that of the historical Gothic.

Gothicized historical novels are generally said to have originated with Thomas Leland's *Longsword, Earl of Salisbury* (1762), although the mixture of history and the Gothic can be traced back still further, to the plays of Shakespeare, particularly *Macbeth*. Certainly the most important (and popular) of the historical Gothics was Clara Reeve's *The Old English Baron* (1778) (originally published in 1777 under the title *The Champion of Virtue*). Reeve declared her intention in *The Old English Baron* was to follow in the footsteps of Walpole's *The Castle of Otranto* (1764) by blending history and romance, while eliminating what she saw as *Otranto*'s excesses. The result was a short novel set in the time of the Wars of the Roses, involving a young peasant who, thanks to prophetic dreams and other revelations, discovers his father's treacherous murder and his own noble birth. Unfortunately, in attempting to correct what she saw as Walpole's defects, Reeve ended up composing a fairly didactic, moralistic novel, which critics and even Walpole himself decried as hopelessly dull. Walpole wrote that the story of the murder was so boring and predictable that nearly any murder trial at the Old Bailey would have provided better fodder for a novel. But notwithstanding these criticisms, readers loved *The Old English Baron*, and it remained in print nearly continuously from its initial publication to the present day.

The popularity of the historical Gothic persisted for a number of years after Reeve published *The Old English Baron*; among the most important of these novels were Sophia Lee's *The Recess* (1783-85) and Anne Fuller's *Alan Fitz-Osborne* (1786). That Palmer was influenced tremendously by these novels is apparent not only from the plot of his novel, but also from the naming of his characters. *The Old English Baron*'s evil Baron Fitz-Owen lends variations of his name to Palmer's Lord Fitzallan and the servant Owen; Palmer's Edmund also takes his name from *Old English Baron*, while Emma and Montmorenci owe their names to Miss Lee's *The Recess*.

Palmer sets his novel in the time of Edward III, a tumultuous period in the history of England. At a young age, Edward III succeeded his father, Edward II, who was murdered, apparently at the instigation of his wife Isabella and her consort Mortimer. At age eighteen, he revolted against his mother's control, banishing her from the court and executing Mortimer. The rest of his long reign, which lasted a total of fifty years, was spent largely in various wars.

The early years of Edward's rule were marked by conflicts with Scotland. In 1328, in the Treaty of Northampton, Edward renounced his claim to the Scottish throne, but soon came to resent the terms of the treaty, and supported Edward Baliol against the Scottish king, David II (David Bruce). The wars with Scotland persisted for a number of years and were never fully settled, before trouble with France came to divide Edward's attention.

Edward, angered over disputes concerning English holdings in France, and at French support of the Scots, launched England into what came to be known as the Hundred Years War in 1337. Wars with the Scots and the French continued throughout Edward's long reign, and remained unresolved at his death in 1377.

Of course, as Shakespeare did with his histories, Palmer is forced to condense a number of historical events which unfolded over a period of years or decades into a few pages in order to make his narrative concise and interesting. Ultimately, however, although Palmer devotes quite a lot of time to it in the novel, the historical accounts are of fairly little importance to the reader (either contemporary or modern), who is more interested in the exploits of the hero Leonard and his friends.

The novel, as we have noted, is part history and part romance. It was, as mentioned above, inspired by *The Old English Baron* and other early historical Gothic novels. But a more significant, and certainly more uncommon influence, is that of Cervantes's masterpiece, *Don Quixote*. Like that novel, *Mystery of the Black Tower* is principally the story of a knight-errant seeking to win himself fame and renown, accompanied by his loquacious and cowardly servant. Of course, Leonard shares few personality traits with Don Quixote, since it would not do for the noble hero of a Gothic romance to be delusional and chase windmills, but Owen is very clearly modelled after Sancho Panza. Like his forbear, Owen talks boldly, but acts cowardly whenever danger presents itself; like Sancho, too, Owen spends most of his time complaining of thirst and hunger and decrying the hard life of a knight-errant.

Notably, though the book is entitled *Mystery of the Black Tower*, the episode with the Black Tower actually occupies very little of the book, and, in reality, is not overly mysterious. The novel's plot is instead filled with digressions, with Leonard and Owen constantly meeting intriguing characters along the way, such as a hermit, a fisherman, and a banditti chieftain, who relate the sad and often horrifying events of their pasts. Despite (or perhaps due to) the fact that the narrative is somewhat disjointed, winding, and digressive, the novel manages to retain the reader's interest throughout, and although by the end of the novel, every character seems to have gone through so many identity changes that it's difficult to recall exactly who is who, none of that really seems to matter. The tale is constantly engrossing, the only weak point of the narrative being perhaps the unnecessarily long descriptions of 14th century English and Scottish politics.

Besides its interest in its own right, Professor Frank points out another reason why *Mystery of the Black Tower* is a significant work. Following its publication, it touched off a wave of Gothic novels involving towers or turrets, so many, in fact, that Frank, in

The First Gothics, devotes an entire Gothic subcategory to the "tower or turret Gothic." Among the works clearly inspired by *Mystery of the Black Tower* include G. D. Hernon's *Louisa, or the Black Tower* (1805), William Herbert and Edward Wedlake Brayley's *Syr Reginalde, or, the Black Tower* (1803), and perhaps even William Harrison Ainsworth's historical romance *The Tower of London* (1840).

Although it may be a fairly formulaic tale, *The Mystery of the Black Tower* manages to distinguish itself from the majority of the other minor Gothics published during the period through Palmer's engaging, and often humorous prose, and his obvious gifts as a storyteller. It is, then, with great pleasure that Valancourt Books presents *The Mystery of the Black Tower*, not doubting that our subscribers will find the book just as enjoyable as Palmer's did more than two centuries ago.

JAMES D. JENKINS
CHICAGO, July 2005

NOTE ON THE TEXT

The text of the Valancourt Books edition of *The Mystery of the Black Tower* is based on that of the first edition, which was printed for the author in two volumes at the Minerva Press, London, in 1796. It was sufficiently popular in its day to be translated into French, as *Les Mystères de la Tour Noire, roman traduit de l'anglais de Jh. Palmer, célèbre acteur de Londres,* and published at Paris, Chez Roux, during An VII of the revolutionary calendar (1799).

The text of the first edition presents a number of problems for a modern editor. Many words are misspelled, sometimes consistently, and sometimes not. Some errors are clearly intentional, and are intended to reproduce English as Palmer must have believed it was written in the time of Edward III (e.g., "frantick," "domestick," "sate" as the preterite of "sit," and "eat" rather than "ate" as the preterite of the verb "to eat.") Some are apparently Palmer's errors of usage, such as "ought" instead of "aught."

While in general I opted to reproduce the spelling and punctuation of the first edition, I did elect to change a number of obvious errors: "intrim" for "interim," "zehyr" for "zephyr," "tastless" for "tasteless," "stoped" for "stopped," "rabbet" for "rabbit," "Gorgeon" for "Gorgon," and "draged" for "dragged," to name a few. Where the error was consistently made (either by Palmer, or by 18th century writers in general), I have retained the incorrect spellings, as "ideot" for "idiot," "controul" for "control," "stupified" for "stupefied," and "villany" for "villainy," to give but a few examples. The resulting text is a compromise between competing interests, namely, the desire not to confuse modern readers unfamiliar with perusing two hundred year old texts, while still preserving the spirit of the original book.

Finally, I would like to acknowledge Jessica Albano of the University of Washington Libraries for her kind assistance.

THE
MYSTERY

OF THE

𝕭𝕷𝕬𝕮𝕶 𝕿𝕺𝕸𝕰𝕽,

A ROMANCE,

BY

JOHN PALMER, Jun.

AUTHOR OF THE

HAUNTED CAVERN.

Can fuch things be,
And overcome us like a fummer's cloud,
Without our fpecial wonder? You make me ftrange
Ev'n to the difpofition that I owe,
When now I think, you can behold fuch fights,
And keep the natural ruby of your cheeks,
When mine is blanch'd with fear.

SHAKESPEARE.

VOL I.

LONDON:

PRINTED FOR THE AUTHOR,
BY WILLIAM LANE,
AT THE
𝔐inerva=Prefs,
LEADENHALL-STREET.

M.DCC.XCVI.

DEDICATION

TO

MRS. VERNON,

MY DEAR MADAM,

WHEN I first requested permission to inscribe the follow-ing work to you, the partiality of your friendship led you to think, that my own interest should urge me rather to seek the sanction of a higher name: but, surely, an author may be allowed the privilege of chusing his own patron, and dedications be a tribute to private worth, as well as the meed of public desert.

As a wife, and as a mother, Mrs. Vernon has ever been a pattern of all that is praise-worthy and good; and, left a widow, she has reared a numerous offspring to honour, by instilling into the breasts of her daughters the lessons of truth, and of prudence; and inspiring her sons with every sentiment of manly virtue. Those sons now stand forward, as soldiers, to defend the rights of their country; may they return, crowned with conquest, and hailed by the applause of their countrymen, to bless a parent, to whom they are so much indebted!

Beyond all this, the particular obligations which I am under to you, demand every grateful return I can make, and the following pages are all I have to offer: not that I have vanity enough to imagine this dedication will add

1

much celebrity to your name: should the story itself charm an anxious hour, it is all I dare hope. If, however, "*The Mystery of the Black Tower*," be stamped with public approbation, it will remain a lasting memorial of that unalterable affection and esteem, with which I am,

My dear Madam,

Your very sincere,

and faithful servant,

JOHN PALMER, Jun.

THE

M Y S T E R Y

OF THE

Black Tower

CHAPTER I

Yet why should Man, mistaken, deem it nobler
To dwell in palaces, and high-roof'd halls,
Than in God's forests, Architect supreme!
Say, is the Persian carpet, than the fields
Or meadows mantle gay, more richly wov'n;
Or softer to the votaries of ease
Than bladed grass—perfum'd with dew-drop flow'rs!

WHARTON.

He prefer'd me
Above the maidens of my age and rank;
Still shun'd their company, and still sought mine.
I was not won by gifts, yet still he gave;
And all his gifts, tho' small, yet spoke his love:
He pick'd the earliest strawberries in the woods,
The cluster'd filberts, and the purple grapes:
He taught a prating stare to speak my name;
And when he found a nest of nightingales,
Or callow linnets, he would shew 'em me,
And let me take 'em out.

DRYDEN.

DURING the reign of the illustrious Edward of Windsor, the scourge of Gallia, and whose warlike arm plucked from her pallid sons fresh leaves of laurel, which he entwined in England's diadem; a peasant, named Christopher, resided in a beautiful valley in Northumberland, from which the golden rays of Phœbus were excluded by the impervious branches of a hanging wood, that environed it, and cast a delightful shade upon the plain beneath.

Christopher's family was composed of a wife and son: Leonard, so was the latter called, had not attained his twentieth year; the down of manhood was scarcely spread over his countenance, yet were his limbs athletic, and his constitution hardy; in short, he was formed for the service of Mars, though to face the nightly wolf, or drive the banditti from the vale, was all he knew of war, save the instructions he received from his father, who had spent his spring of life in the service of his country, and now strove to impress the mind of his offspring with the desire of arms.

In love, Leonard was a greater adept; his heart had long been captured by the charms of Emma, daughter of a neighbouring hind, who returned his love with interest; and unacquainted with the little arts practised by too many of her sex, she frankly owned he possessed her affection. Their mutual passion had not, however, escaped the penetrating eye of Christopher, and his wife Barbara, who forbade their son to encourage it. He promised never to call her his without their approbation; but at the same time refused to discontinue his addresses to her: he thought their commands unjust.

"Is she not," he would say to himself, "my equal in point of condition? In personal endowments how far my superior: I will not scorn the mandate of my parents, but to cease loving and to see her is impossible."

While Emma was tending her flock, Leonard generally amused himself with flinging the bar, shooting at a mark, or some such manly exercise. One evening, while he was employed in the latter diversion, his mistress exclaimed, "Is it possible your heart can be susceptible of love? You never appear so much inspired as when you are wrestling with the swains, then you are happy; but when with me, you are obliged to seek society in your bow and arrows."

"Does my Emma," replied the youth, "censure me for endeavouring to render myself worthy of her? My present humble estate does not entitle me to the blessing of your hand; it were to place the diamond from the eye of day; my aim must therefore be to acquire that fortune, which but for your sake I should despise."

She was about to make an answer, when Christopher joined them, and put an end to their discourse.

"So, sir," he cried, "here you are at your usual vocation: but you must now prepare for other wars, than those on foolish damsel's hearts: follow me home immediately."

With these words he sullenly departed; and, while Leonard remained pondering on his speech, the sound of a trumpet, for the first time, pierced his ear, and made the blood fly mantling to his cheek: forgetful of his fair companion, he ran towards the castle, which was situated on an eminence of the eastern hill, and commanded a view of the spacious ocean that laved the base of the cliff whereon it reared its towering head. The God of day, who was rapidly descending beneath the opposite wood, cast his bright influence on the battlements, that shewed themselves above the trees, and gave a burning polish to them. He entered the courtyard, which was filled with armed men; their glittering helmets, and their towering plumes, caused him to eye the warriors with wonder; and admiration fixed him to the spot, till recollecting he had come thither uninvited, he hastily withdrew, and in his return met Emma, driving her flock homeward. He instantly joined her, and saw her safe to the portal of her father's dwelling.

By this time the mist of night was diffused over the face of earth, and nought was heard, save the screeching sounds of the moping owl, or plaintive notes of the mournful nightingale.

Leonard was bending his way homeward, when his steps were arrested by a light that issued from an apartment in the northern tower of the castle, which was reported to be the abode of some disembodied spirit, and was known by the appellation of the Black Tower. There was, indeed, a mystery entailed on the mansion, which he could never penetrate: often had he questioned Christopher on the subject, but to no purpose, he was always silenced, and still remained perplexed in the mazes of conjecture. In the chamber before-mentioned, (which was entirely shut up and useless) lights had been frequently seen by the inhabitants of the vale, which caused them to be considered as the work of some supernatural agency.

Repairing to his own cottage, he was much surprised to find old Barbara in tears.

"What," said the youth, "my beloved mother, is the cause of this your grief?"

"Alas!" she replied, "I have too much cause. Know you not that our Lord Fitzallan has authorized this strange Baron, who is just arrived, to raise troops amongst his vassals? Twenty are to go; who they are, poor unfortunate souls, the lots will determine: you may possibly be amongst them, and we shall lose the prop of our declining years."

Leonard's eyes flashed with joy. "And do you weep for this?" he cried, "Restrain your briny sorrow, and fear not but heaven will restore me to you. Now that one half of Europe is in arms, how inglorious must be that man's soul, who, unrestrained by age, burns not to join the warlike conflict."

"Oh nature! thou wilt break forth!" cried Barbara, turning her eyes towards heaven, while scalding drops rolled through the furrows of her aged cheek, as the cataract rushes down the rugged mountain's side.

"No more of this ridiculous whining!" exclaimed Christopher, "the cause is a good one: I have often fought these Scots, and know their courage to be as hardy as their element. No honour can be lost by combating them, though much is to be gained; nor is the brave Baron De Courci, under whose banner you serve, a Knight who will suffer valour to go unrewarded.

Therefore boy hold yourself in readiness, and pray it may be your destiny to follow him."

Supper was now produced, of which Leonard eat sparingly; the occurrences of the evening ran strongly in his mind, and deprived him of appetite. He retired to rest, but for a long time could not entice the balmy power of sleep, and when he dropped into a slumber, his dreams presented the warriors he had seen: he fought battles in imagination, and was awakened by the fancied noise of the shrill trumpet. Thus he passed the night, and no sooner was the veil of darkness removed to the other world, than he arose, and, having equipped himself in his best doublet, he sat at the window watching for the moment which was to determine his stay or go, racked by anxiety. At length the sounds of martial musick echoed from the castle, on which he rushed from the cottage, and was joined by the inhabitants of the dale. Soon after the troops appeared, issuing from the leafy labyrinth, headed by the Baron De Courci and his son.

Instantly the drawing of the lots commenced; but no pen can do justice to the countenance of Leonard, on finding himself doomed to remain at home: his features, that were before animated by hope, were now contracted, and disappointment lowered his brow, as the dark thunder cloud suddenly envelopes the blue and concave firmament.

The Baron noticed his agitation. "What," said he, "young man, occasions your disorder?"

"My Lord," replied the youthful peasant, "I would be a soldier: I have tarried in this peaceful spot too long; my country demands my arm, and I cannot refrain from accusing fate, who has prevented my accompanying you to the field of glory."

"And what, my friend," cried De Courci, speaking to one, whom fortune, willing to evince her blindness, had dubbed soldier, "What is the cause of thy despondency?"

7

"Truly, my Lord," he returned, "I am no miser: I do not covet the glory my friend talks of, and will, with pleasure, resign my share to him."

Leonard's heart dilated with rapture, and the cowardice of this reptile, for which, on any other occasion, he would have spurned him, was lost in the hope of obtaining his post.

"My Lord," he exclaimed, "will you deign to accept my services in lieu of his? I will serve you faithfully!"

"I will be sworn thou wilt," quoth De Courci, "thou wilt add honour to my followers, who would be disgraced by the company of yon paltroon. Let those who are allotted soldiers follow me."

He marched to the Castle of Fitzallan, attended by his new troops, with whom he proceeded to the armoury, where they quickly caparisoned themselves. The son of Christopher being equipped, was about to depart, but was stopped by the Baron.

"Hold!" cried he, presenting him with a sword richly studded, "Already I feel an interest in your behalf: receive this as an earnest of my future favour."

"Excuse me, my Lord," replied Leonard, "I am unworthy of such honour: this I am about to wear is good enough. When I have rusted it in the blood of England's enemies, I may claim a better."

"True," said Lord De Courci, "but wear this for me, and if you consider it as an obligation, repay me by making a brave use of it. To-morrow, by early dawn, we depart for the borders."

Leonard bowing, took his leave, and hastened to the spot where Emma constantly tended her sheep, secretly vowing to spill his last blood in service of so gallant a leader. The timid maid shrieked at the sight of him.

"Do you not know me?" said the peasant, raising his beaver.

"Oh, Heavens!" she cried, "Is it my Leonard? Then my fears are true!"

"I foresaw this meeting," he replied, "and painful it is to me. But hear, nor vainly seek to put me from my purpose. I cannot resolve to spend my life in this sequestered place, to die unknown, and unregretted: though humbly born, I wish my name may descend into posterity; to convince the world it is not the splendid title, or gaudy ermine of an Emperor, can constitute true greatness, unless when backed by real worth; otherwise he is more abject than his meanest subject, and his boasted grandeur serves but to unveil his failings, and make them more conspicuous. The happy chance I have long wished for, is arrived, and though parting with you will much embitter it, yet, should my heart strings crack, I will not quit my design."

"Go then," quoth the maid, "but, oh! forget not Emma."

"Impossible! while life continues, you will be certain of my tenderest thoughts."

"Farewell!" she said, "may Heaven preserve you!"

The tears, at these words, stood trembling on her cheek like morning dew upon the opening lily.

"No more," exclaimed Leonard, "fear not my safety; and for my love, I call each heavenly power to witness this my vow. No time shall ever diminish the fervour of my passion, or other beauties make me forget the object of it. Adieu, remember me in your oraisons."

He pressed her hand to his lips, and, tearing himself away, repaired homeward, where his feelings were again rouzed by the grief of Barbara.

"Unfeeling boy!" cried the old woman, "you will break my heart: the lot fell not to you, yet you must wilfully run your head in danger."

"Cease mother!" answered her son, "nor wound me by the sight of your sorrow: something tells me I shall return to bless your aged arms: the life of a peasant I cannot brook, and I would rather die in honour, than live in poor obscurity!"

"Enough," quoth Christopher, "I commend thy valour."

He then drew from his pocket a miniature richly set. "Wear this within your bosom," continued he, "treasure it as your existence, nor lose it as you value your future happiness."

Leonard took it with astonishment, and found it was the portrait of a Knight: the back of the picture was much disfigured, and appeared as if some characters had been scratched thereon; not one letter, however, could he distinguish.

"Ask me no questions," said the old man, observing he was about to speak, "you will know more hereafter. Once more I conjure you to be careful of my gift."

The youth promised he would not be separated from it, but with his life. They shortly after parted for the night; but Leonard could not close his eye-lids: the mystery of the portrait he had received: the sudden change in his situation, employed his thoughts, and forbade his enjoying the renovating power of sleep.

He arose, 'ere the first tints of Aurora enlightened the eastern horizon, and buckled on his armour: long he did not tarry before he perceived the troops issue from the wood into the valley; on which he descended from the chamber, and took leave of his parents. His parting was tender and respectful; he embraced them both with an unfeigned ardour, and the tear of filial affection trembled in his eye, as he received their benediction.

In the plain he found the Lord De Courci. "Come, my young friend," he cried, "we tarry for you."

The peasant having apologized for his absence, mounted his horse, and the Baron caused him to ride on one side of himself, treating him with the condescending familiarity of an equal. In their course they passed the dwelling of Emma, who sat at the window pale and weeping. Leonard kissed his hand to her, which she returned, and followed him with her eyes, till the envious woods concealed him from her view; she thought, perhaps, for ever!

CHAPTER II

Had some brave chief this martial scene beheld,
By Pallas guarded through the dreadful field;
Might darts be bid to turn their points away,
And swords around him innocently play;
The war's whole art with wonder had he seen,
And counted heroes where he counted men:

POPE.

THEY commenced their progress northward: during their
march, Leonard frequently turned his head, and viewed the
soldiers, with an enthusiastic delight, as the sun-beams danced
upon their glossy crests, and gave them an appearance more
than mortal.

"Tell me, my young friend," said the Baron, as they proceeded, "how came the love of arms so strongly to possess you?
In the sequestered spot, where you have passed your time, I
should have imagined no thought, save that of peace, would
have possessed you."

"Since my Lord deigns to ask," replied the youth, "he shall
know the cause. Some four years since, it was I think on the
eve of Christmas, as the peasants of our valley were regaling
themselves, and wiling away the time in innocent pleasures, an
aged minstrel arrived amongst them. I was at the time a boy,
but the verses of the bard can never be blotted from my recollection: he sung of the Grecian and Trojan heroes; of the virtues
and sufferings of the illustrious Alfred, and concluded with the
valour and heroism of the renowned Coeur de Lion. His words
touched my very heart, and the manly firmness with which he
struck the trembling strings, fired my youthful mind: from that
time my rustic sports, and employments, were neglected, and,
as far as in my power lay, I strove to qualify myself for the
distinguished character of a soldier."

11

"That you will be a good one," quoth De Courci, "I prognosticate." Then turning to his son, "admit this young stranger to your confidence, he deserves, or I am much deceived, your warmest esteem."

Edgar, so was his offspring called, congratulated his new acquaintance on the many happy days he hoped they should pass together; while Leonard, overpowered by gratitude, could only bow in silence for the unmerited generosity he experienced.

Here it may not be improper to give a brief abstract of the occasion of the war, in which they were about to engage.

On the coronation of Edward the Third, the subjects of Gallia, who had been apprehended in England, were emancipated; and as Charles, the French King, had entered in the business, merely to forward the designs of his sister, the consort of Edward of Caernarvon, and that being obtained, a peace was instantly concluded. The Scots, however, who had no connection with the Queen, resolved to avail themselves of the distracted state into which their neighbour kingdom was at that time plunged. They therefore attempted to surprise the castle of Norham, in which they were frustrated, by the vigilance of Sir Robert Mannours, the Governor. The English Consul instantly sent Ambassadors to Robert Bruce, the Caledonian Sovereign, to complain of the breach of the treaty which had taken place, and also to treat about a final pacification. That active Prince, however, whose life had been employed in efforts to throw off the English yoke, avowed his determination not to miss so favourable an opportunity of annoying the enemies of his country: he also sent a solemn defiance, adding, that it was his design forthwith to invade England. This the ministry hoped to prevent, by proposing to appoint commissioners to meet on the marches, and treat about a lasting amnesty; to which he consented, but at the same time, continued inflexible as to the threatened invasion; and a body of troops were in-

12

stantly raised under the Earl of Murray and Lord Douglas. Edward, even at so early a period, discovered those sparks of valour, which, at a riper age, burst into a flame: he repaired to Durham, where his forces joined him, and where he learned the Scots had passed the Tyne, and ravaged the eastern parts of the Bishopric; on which he thought of intercepting them in their retreat; and, dividing his army, commenced his march in quest of the enemy: but after suffering severe fatigue, and excessive difficulties, through woods, mountains and morasses, and discovering no traces of them, but by the smoke of several villages they had fired, he turned his course towards the Tyne, and arrived at the place where the Scots had crossed: as it was natural to suppose they would return the same way, he took possession of the northern side.

Douglas, who had intimation of his motions, posted his followers in an advantageous situation, till he should receive more certain advice of his adversaries' strength. In the mean time the King of England marched down the river, proclaiming, that whosoever discovered where the Scottish army were encamped, should have the honour of Knighthood bestowed on him, together with an hundred marks a year, as a recompense. Soon he received the wished for tidings from one, who, lured by this promise, had made excursions, and found the enemy at three miles distance, on the other side the Ware, that laves the base of a gigantic hill, whereon they were encamped.

Edward advanced against them, but the stupendous stones which lay on the bed of the river, and the current, which was so rapid, from the rain which had just fallen, rendered it impracticable to pass with any prospect of success: for, besides these obstructions, the Scots were ranged in order on the declivity of the mountain. On this he sent an herald to inform them, if they were inclined to come to an engagement, he would retire, and allow them to cross the Ware; or if they would fall back to a certain distance, he would pass the river, and give them battle. The Scottish general sent him for answer, that he was not so impolitic as to follow the advice of a foe.

Thus did the armies face each other, till Douglas, finding his provender was almost expended, decamped at midnight, and, marching some miles higher up the river, took possession of an hill, flanked by a wood; and Edward was no sooner informed of his retreat, than he followed, and posted himself upon a mountain, opposite his antagonist, who, while they were thus situated, forded the river, and, entering the English camp, by favour of the night, penetrated as far as the royal tent, with intention to carry off the King; but the guards suddenly surrounded the Caledonian chief, who, with infinite valour, cut his way through those who opposed him, and made his escape.

The Scots, enriched with plunder, now thought of returning to their native country, and an accident hastened their design. A Knight of their army being captured, was interrogated by Edward, to whom he declared that the troops of Douglas had orders to be ready armed at night. The English, well knowing the enterprizing spirit of that Baron, imagined he again meant to attack them under covert of darkness, and resolved to give him a warm reception: they, therefore, drew themselves up in order of battle, and continued so till morning, while the enemy retired in silence, under favour of the adjoining grove; and, passing a large morass, conducted their enterprize with such precipitancy, that by dawn they had made a considerable progress, and the next day reached their own country, laden with booty.

Edward, on the scouts bringing him intelligence of their departure, was much mortified to be thus baffled in his first campaign, and retired to Durham, from whence he proceeded to York, at which place he dismissed the great part of his followers.

On his return from this expedition, the melancholy tidings of his father's murder, first reached his ear, which he bewailed with unfeigned affliction.

The English and Scottish commissioners now opened their conference, and a treaty was concluded on terms highly advantageous to the latter, but which reflected shame on Edward, as in it he resigned all pretensions to a kingdom, which had cost his noble Grandsire so much pains to subdue. It was also farther stipulated, that the English Barons should be restored to the estates they had formerly held in Caledonia; notwithstanding which, several nobles were still debarred of their right. Their Sovereign, therefore, interposed with the regency of Scotland (Robert Bruce being now dead) in their behalf, from whom he received nought but evasive answers: he had, besides, another cause of complaint, for that they had seized upon the town of Upsetlington, which, although situated on the north of the river Tweed, belonged to the Bishopric of Durham. Edward, glad to avail himself of any pretence for renouncing a league so dishonourable to him, and which tarnished one of the brightest characters that ever graced the pages of our British annals! but as he had promised the Pope, on bond, not to molest Scotland for a certain space of time, he feared to take any measures, by which he might be compelled to forfeit the obligation. The Barons, however, whose interests were more immediately concerned than their Royal Master's, resolved, by force of arms, to take possession of what their enemies so unjustly withheld: they therefore had recourse to Edward Baliol, (son of John Baliol) who, at his father's demise, had been left a captive at the court of England. They encouraged him to endeavour at regaining the crown of his parent, vowing, their lives and fortunes should be spent in his service. Being a Prince of an enterprizing disposition, and a vast share of ambition, he accepted their proffered aid, levied forces, embarked at Ravenspur in Yorkshire, and landed at Kinghorn, where he routed the followers of Sir Alexander Seton, and slew that leader.

From thence he proceeded towards Glandmuir, where the Earl of Marr was encamped, with a numerous army, while an advanced body was stationed to oppose the progress of the English. Confiding in their numbers, and the depth of the river which lay between the contending parties, they lay in a careless manner almost unguarded. This was imparted to Baliol, and, a ford being discovered, he crossed it in the night, with the whole of his troops, and discomfited the enemy.

The Earl of Marr, who, with his forces, was at some miles distance, proposed to starve the English out: the expedient, however, was looked upon by Robert, Earl of Carrick, as the cool dictates of cowardice, and as such he proclaimed it, which so incensed the ferocious chief, that he prepared to give instant battle to his opponents; and such was the confusion with which he made his attack, that in passing over a narrow defile, men and horses fell over each other, and became an easy prey to the English, who made a terrible slaughter. The two leaders were slain, with a great number of Knights, and about thirteen thousand soldiers, while Baliol's loss was trifling, who then entered Perth, which he put in a posture of defence, and where he was shortly besieged by Archibald Douglas and the Earl of Dunbar.

While these transactions took place in the north, the English fleet, which lay in Berwick harbour, gained a compleat victory over a Flemish squadron, that had been employed by the Scots to attack them; and these repeated conquests so intimidated the foes of Baliol, they thought all farther opposition vain, and he was therefore crowned at Scone.

In the mean time, David Bruce, son to the late Robert, with Jane, the sister of England's King, to whom he had been affianced, were sent to France, and graciously received there by Philip de Valois.

Soon after Edward, and the new Caledonian Monarch, had an interview, at which the latter did homage for the kingdom of Scotland; obliged himself to pay yearly two thousand pounds, and to furnish the English with a certain number of troops in time of war.

Baliol, in leaving Perth, was attacked by Murray, whom he defeated, and made captive. Then, thinking himself secure in the submission of his subjects and also in a truce which had been concluded, he dismissed Edward's troops, and repaired to Annah, where he proposed to hold his Parliament. The Brussian party, however, thought to avail themselves of this opportunity to seize him, and his adherents, and their scheme was executed with such secresy, that he had scarce time to mount his horse, with which he escaped to Carlisle, while his followers fell into the hands of their enemies; and his brother, after having performed miracles of valour, resigned his life. The Scots, intoxicated with success, entered Cumberland, which they ravaged, and gave our English Edward a pretence to declare openly for Baliol. He therefore complained of these hostilities, and sent ambassadors to exact homage from David Bruce, which being boldly refused, war was denounced against him, as a contumacious vassal: he immediately therefore collected his forces, and marched to Newcastle upon Tyne, which was fixed for the rendezvous, and where Leonard joined him. The appearance of the camp, together with the martial noise that issued from the same, made the heart of Leonard dance with rapture in his breast, and he languished for the moment when the trumpet's clangour should summon him to combat.

Edward now took his course to Berwick, which he laid siege to, but the place was strongly garrisoned, under two of the bravest Scottish chiefs, Patrick Dunbar, and Sir William De Keith, the governor, who made such a gallant defence, that the King of England was fain to turn the siege into a blockade by sea and land, and to penetrate farther into the country. He accordingly proceeded as far as Edinburgh, free from opposition, save that he was at times harassed by the troops of Douglas, who prudently avoided a decisive battle; and, after a tedious unavailing peregrination through the enemies land, from which the natives had conveyed their valuable effects, he returned to Berwick, and carried on his operations there with redoubled vigour; nor could he be diverted from his purpose, although Douglas had entered England, and invested the castle of Banborough, which contained the person of the Queen.

Edward knew the place to be well fortified, and, being as great a politician as he was a warrior, looked upon this as an artifice, to draw him from the enterprize, and he now resolved to reduce the town at all events. The Scots, however, protected themselves with astonishing valour, until their works being nearly destroyed, they demanded a five day's truce, on condition, that if they received no succours during that period, the town should be surrendered.

Sir William De Keith, by some manœuvre, then reached the camp of Douglas, whom he persuaded to hasten to the relief of Berwick. With a numerous force they arrived at Bothville, near Halidowns Hill, and drew up their army in four battalions. The English were situated on an eminence, in four divisions also, flanked with archers. Here did Edward wait the enemy's charge, who ascended the hill at the hour of vespers. Their career, however, was soon stopped by the resistance they met with, and their heavy armour, which deprived them of breath; they were also much galled by the arrows, which the English bow-men let fly in showers at them, and the huge stones that were hurled down upon them, did dreadful execution. During the battle, Leonard encountered Douglas, and after a well contested combat, stretched himself lifeless on the field of battle. De Courci had observed all this, and as the eagle, with joy, beholds it's young one's wings first expanded to the sun, so did the Baron glow with transport, on finding his bounteous goodness had not been lavished on one undeserving it. He approached, and congratulated the youth on his maiden effort in arms. The peasant, however, tarried not to hear his eulogium, but, rushing into the midst of the enemy, dealt destruction round him; and the death of their general being by this time known, the Scots fell into disorder and dismay, on which Edward ordered Lord Darcy, with a body of light armed foot, to attack them in the flank, while he himself, at the head of a choice brigade of men at arms, and archers, fell in among them. All resistance was now at an end, and a dreadful slaughter ensued. This important victory cost the English only one Knight, one Esquire, and thirteen foot soldiers, and the castle of Berwick surrendered on the next morning. Edward, who had observed the party under De Courci's command, to be particularly active, considered himself indebted to that noble for his triumph, and, therefore, summoned him to his presence: for that great Monarch, after the business of the war, was as anxious to reward those who merited it, as he was vigorous during the battle.

CHAPTER III

Oh witness Heaven!
Whose eye the heart's profoundest depth explores,
That if not to perform my regal task;
To be the common father of my people,
Patron of honour, virtue, and religion;
If not to shelter useful worth, to guard
His well-earn'd portion from the sons of rapine,
And deal out justice with impartial hand;
If not to spread on all good men my bounty,
The treasures trusted to me, not my own;
If not to raise anew the English name,
By peaceful arts that grace the land they bless,
And generous war, to humble proud oppressors:
Yet more, if not to build the public weal
On that firm base, which can alone resist
Both time and chance, fair liberty and law;
If I for these great ends am not ordain'd—
May I ne'er poorly fill the throne of England.

MALLET.

DE COURCI, and his followers, entered Berwick, amidst the acclamations of their fellow soldiers, which accompanied them even to the castle, where the royal Edward courteously received them, and expressed aloud his obligation for the service the Baron had rendered him.

"Not to me, dread Liege," replied that noble, "you owe the victory, but to my followers; particularly to the single arm of a bold stripling, who seemed desirous to leave his body in the field, for wherever danger appeared thickest, I saw him carving his way to glory, while the enemies darts flew numerous round his head, and his shield shewed like a pigmy forest."

"Who is it?" said the King, "that is thus worthy of your praise?"

"A low-born youth," returned De Courci, "who merited a higher birth."

20

"His birth," quoth the Monarch, "would be to us at least his recommendation: it is the duty of a Sovereign to reward the deserving; and though I confess honours are too frequently purchased by gold, yet sure a Prince cannot feel so much satisfaction, as when he barters them for the affection of a loyal subject. But produce your hero."

The Baron took Leonard by the hand, and presented him to Edward, who thus addressed him.

"Welcome to my presence; smile at the frowns of fortune, and be it my care to make atonement for her envy. Thus I create you Knight."

The young peasant retreated a few steps, saying, "Your Majesty's goodness is too great; to the partiality of my Lord De Courci I am indebted for it. Believe me, Sire, I only did my duty; what thousands did that now lie breathless on the plain. If it is your will to reward the valiant, the son of that great man deserves your utmost bounty: be the honours you intended for your lowly slave, transfered to him, while I return to that obscurity, from which the Baron's fostering hand has raised me."

"Thou art as generous as brave," replied the King. "My Lord De Courci, let me see your son." Edgar stepped forth, and Edward thus continued. "You have witnessed the conduct of this excellent young man, who has refused the gift which he asserts is your's. The example of generosity is set me by one of my subjects, and I joyfully profit by it; kneel therefore both, and take the reward of your valour," then laying his sword upon their shoulders, "Arise, my Knights of the battle," he continued, "moreover to support your dignities, one thousand marks are annually yours: nor think my gratitude here shall make a pause—no, my actions shall tell how much I still consider myself your debtor."

They accepted the liberality of their Sovereign with diffi-
dence, and returned their illustrious Monarch the thanks that
were his due.

Edward, having thus annexed Berwick to the crown of
England, punctually adhered to the articles of capitulation; he
permitted the Scots to remove their effects, and suffered those,
who were disposed to take the oath of allegiance, to remain:
then, having left six thousand men with Baliol, he returned to
the metropolis, and De Courci, with his son, and Leonard,
having tarried at court some days, set out for the castle of the
former, which was situated in the west of England. On the
second evening they descried the stately mansion; it was
strongly fortified, and surrounded by a deep moat. The bugle-
horn being sounded, the draw-bridge was instantly let down,
and they entered the court-yard, where they dismounted, and
from thence the Baron led them to the apartment of his lady.
She received De Courci, not with the accustomed ardency of
conjugal affection, but with an assumed tenderness. Edgar she
scarcely noticed, but to Leonard she was profuse in her compliments, and he returned her courtesy with a dignified
complacency, which he possessed in an eminent degree. Indeed, she had ever evinced a strong antipathy against the
offspring of her Lord, (for Edgar was the fruit of a former alliance,) and possessed all the implacable hatred that too often
marks the character of a step-dame.

The friendship that subsisted between the son of Christopher, and young De Courci, was as sincere as that recorded of
Pylades and Orestes; it was strongly cemented by mutual merit,
and the foundation was a lasting one, it was built on the solid
basis of honour and integrity.

Here it may not be improper to give a slight sketch of the
persons and dispositions of these young warriors.

Edgar was of a tall commanding figure: his limbs were
strong, but at the same time lightly formed; his countenance

was expressive, his temper placid, his manners engaging, and his courage undaunted.

Leonard was a larger, and more muscular man; of a dark complexion, and hair, and a penetrating eye: his features, though good, were marked by a ferocity that at first sight rather impressed the mind of the beholder with fear, than any other passion, and was, indeed, an index of his disposition, which although brave to an excess, was tinctured by a head-strong fury that he could not govern. Nevertheless, this failing was but a foil to his numerous virtues; his heart was not unused to the melting mood, nor was his ear or purse ever shut against the story of distress.

He frequently beguiled the morning hours in traversing the adjacent country, while the recollection of his loved Emma, or the perusal of the miniature, given by his father, was the constant companion of his walks. One day, while on his accustomed PEREGRINATION, he was suddenly overtaken by a violent shower of rain, which compelled him to seek shelter in a solitary tattered cottage, at some distance from the residence of De Courci. Therein he found a couple, bending beneath the weight of years, and a youth, about his own age, seated round a scanty peat fire; the latter of whom immediately rose, and resigned his seat to the Knight.

Fortunately for the cottage lad, the rain continued some hours, by which delay he had the happy opportunity of indulging the natural flow of a humorous temper: being blessed with a redundancy of words, and a rapid stream of spirits, he soon had the good chance, not only to entertain his guest, and to extort from him loud and repeated bursts of laughter, but, by the keenness of his wit, procured reward and promotion, as well as esteem and approbation; for Leonard, before he departed, presented him with some pieces of gold, on consideration he should provide himself with new apparel, and repair to the castle.

On his first arrival there, he had the good fortune to please the Lord De Courci, to whom he was presented: from that time he was looked upon as the 'Squire of Leonard, to whom he soon strongly attached himself, in the bonds of fidelity and affection.

With all these agreeable qualifications, Owen (so was he called) had one considerable failing; he was very timid, or to speak more plainly, was a direct coward. This defect, nevertheless, was totally disregarded by his master, who, though he despised the character of a *paltroon*, still, in the present instance, he leniently attributed the 'Squire's fears to his lack of education. In another he would have spurned at that unavoidable blemish of nature; in the line, however, that his faithful dependent stood, he overlooked it quite, and considered it as a probable cause of future merriment, for he soon received several entertaining feasts from some accidental mishaps that occasionally befel Owen. These disasters were ever sure to be attended by alternate emotions of terror, and ludicrous sallies of wit, that had the most entertaining effect on the spirits of Leonard.

He was of Welch extraction, and like most of that country, he prided himself on the high birth of his ancestors, though to say truth, the most his progenitors could boast, was, that they had each kept their own goat, and toasted their own cheese.

CHAPTER IV

And next to him in malicious envy rode,
Upon a ravenous wolfe, and still did chaw
Between his canker'd teeth a venomous toad,
That all the poyson run about his jaw;
But inwardly he chawed his maw
At neighbour's wealth, that made him ever sad,
For death it was when any good he saw,
But when he heard of harme, he vexed wond'rous glad.

SPENSER.

TWO months elapsed at the castle, without any incident worthy to be recorded; at the expiration of which time, the anniversary of Lady De Courci's birth taking place, a solemn tournament was held. Amongst other nobles who came to break a lance, Lord Edmund Fitzallan arrived the day previous to the ceremony. He was a man in whom every vice was centered; deceitful, cruel, and designing; and nature having given him a fair outside, he more easily concealed the blackness of his soul. Like the gilded snake, he was admired for his exterior perfections; and like that destructive reptile, bore venom and annoyance wheresoever he went. This wretch, whose heart was the abode of envy, could not observe the attention with which the Baron's family treated Leonard, without feeling the influence of that baneful passion. In the evening, as he walked with Edgar and his friend, the conversation turning on the intended tournament, Fitzallan told the latter, he had better postpone his efforts in the lists, to some future period; as to a young man possessed of such a vast share of ambition, an overthrow would be insupportable: "but possibly," he continued, "you build your fame on the renown of your illustrious line of ancestors!"

The face of Leonard glowed with indignation; "I would rather," he said, "acquire credit for chastizing ignorant importance."

Edmund, who amidst all his vices, did not want courage, replied, "Restrain your choler, good youth, or you shall quickly learn in me resides the power to quell your boyish insolence."

The temper of Leonard could brook no more, he instantly unsheathed his weapon; his adversary did the same; their arms were upraised, and they were upon the point of discharging their fury on each other's crest, when Edgar, who had been a silent spectator of all that passed, exclaimed, addressing himself to Fitzallan, "Forbear, my Lord, your behaviour is neither manly or courteous, but more resembles that of a rude bravo: to insult the bosom friend of your host, and then expiate your offence, by making his mansion a scene of blood, ill suits the character of a British Knight."

Leonard, conscious it would be infringing the respect he owed Lord De Courci, there to resent the conduct of Edmund, told him, "The place was by him, now he had time for reflection, held too sacred to be made the mansion of riot and confusion; but that 'ere long he should repent each syllable of his ill-timed satire."

Fitzallan replied, "He reverenced the Earl as much as any man; as a proof, he should defer the dispute to a more convenient opportunity." So saying, with folded arms, and a scowling brow, he slowly paced towards the castle.

Leonard, on being left with Edgar, exclaimed, "Think not, my friend, because I will not violate the duty I owe your noble father, that I shall tamely bear this insolence. No, by heaven, and by my hopes of happiness, I swear he shall severely feel the force of my revenge!"

Young De Courci sought, but in vain, to mitigate the wrath of his impetuous companion, who entered the hall, panting with rage. His eyes, and those of Fitzallan, immediately encountered each other: their looks were expressive of a soul replete with indignation; nor were the luxuries of the banquet, or the soul-subduing lyre of the minstrel, sufficient to repress their rising choler. The sparkling goblet mantled on the festive board; the martial verse, and that of love, were alternately rehearsed, and thus was the night spent, till the hour of rest warning them to retire, they bade adieu, and parted.

The rumour of Leonard's and Fitzallan's *altercation* had spread through the castle, and at length reached the ears of Owen. This honest fellow was just raised to the zenith of high good humour, when the tidings came to his knowledge: the goblet, half raised to his lips, sunk imperceptibly on his knee; and, notwithstanding his having entertained the domestics with the great exploits he had heard of his master, and with what he himself intended to do, he concluded with the most dismal and melancholy exclamation. Just at this doleful period, the 'Squire of Edmund entered the kitchen, with eyes inflamed like the blazing comet, and a sullen rage in his looks, that resembled the fury of the winter's storm.

Stephen, so he was called, sat himself by Leonard's follower, on a bench which adjoined the fire side, while his mouth seemed parched with ire. But what was the effect of anger, Owen attributed to thirst; he good naturedly therefore tendered him the cup, which the other accepted, and dashed it violently against the floor; then, casting a look of disdain, in a voice like thunder he exclaimed, "Thus would I destroy the menial slaves of Leonard the Peasant!"

"Thou darest as well take a bear by the tooth," (cried Owen, retreating gently to the farther end of the bench) "No, if my master were here, he would chastise thee most severely for this unprovoked irreverence: *By the valour of my ancestors!* He would indeed carbanado well thy leathern jerkin!"

"Thou liest knave!" returned Stephen, starting from his seat, and drawing his weapon, "to thy face I tell thee that thou liest, most scurvy carrion!"

"Carrion in thy teeth," retorted Owen, "nay, scores of carrion in thy grumbling paunch, thou cross-grained mungrel!"

Having said thus, he retired some steps backward, and
perceiving his adversary preparing to attack him sword in hand,
and reluctant moreover to shed human blood, by unsheathing
his own, for he wore one *to toast cheese* with; he snatched up a
large log of wood that stood in the chimney corner, and, without yielding to any farther ceremony, hurled the beachen
instrument at the threatening Stephen's head, which took so
true and fatal a direction, that both the log and Fitzallan's
menial champion came together to the ground.

The domestics, who had retired to one corner of the
kitchen, when they perceived the furious brandishing of the
sword, now flew to the assistance of the prostrate bravo, who
was utterly incapable of motion. Owen followed their example,
and, though excessively alarmed, was unable to restrain his
humour on the occasion; looking at his fallen enemy, and
recollecting the scurrilous language he had just received, he
shook his head, and exclaimed, "In sad truth there lie two logs,
but alas! with only one head between them."

At that moment he heard footsteps hastening down stairs,
on which he precipitately took himself from the scene of action,
unwilling any longer to be a spectator of the misfortune his
involuntary courage had occasioned.

The confusion that prevailed below, had created a commotion above, and the person who so hastily descended, was no
other than the young Lord De Courci, who had risen from his
couch, and came to inquire the cause of the disturbance. On
being informed of the quarrel that had taken place, and being
likewise assured Stephen was in fault, he gave orders that the
battered 'Squire should be conveyed to bed, and proper care
taken of him; after which he returned to his chamber, and the
servants of the castle retired to rest.

CHAPTER V

Revenge, at first though sweet,
Bitter 'ere long, back on itself recoils:
Let it, I reek not so it light well aim'd.
MILTON

THE ensuing morn was ushered in by the clash of the cymbol, the voice of the shrill trumpet, and the hollow sound of the kettle drum. Edgar and Leonard, whose impatience for the approaching day had scarce permitted to close their eyes, arose at early dawn.

At noon the lists were opened: the Earl and Countess ascended a throne, raised on steps of alabaster, and covered with a canopy of blue sattin, powder'd with silver stars.

Edgar first appeared mounted on a charger, whose whiteness might have vied with the fleecy lamb, or the snow upon the lofty Alps. His armour was of burnished gold; the joints richly inlaid, and his helmet shaded by a profusion of white feathers: his device was a rising sun, the motto *Surgam*. His gauntlet being thrown down, was instantly removed by the 'Squire of the young Lord Nevil, and the champions having received their lances, took their distance: at the onset, however, Edgar unhorsed his opponent, who being violently bruised, was removed without the barrier.

Next came the Lord Fitzallan, long famed for deeds in war, bestriding a rhone courser, who, as though he had caught the infectious malice of his master, champed the steel bit, and, with his neighing, seemed to mock the rattling drum. Edmund's arms were sable, with plumes of the same doleful hue; upon his target appeared the figure of dire Atè, and under written *Revenge!* His warder being deposited by Stephen, with a self-sufficient air he paraded the ring, as though conscious no one was so hardy as to encounter him. But he was suffered only a short time to exult in that idea; his trumpet was answered, and

29

his gage exchanged by Owen; when Leonard entered the ring, upon a steed whose skin was dark and bright as the plumage of the raven: he wore armour of polished steel; on his shield he bore a lion rampant, with this motto, "*Amor Gloriæ,*" and the crimson horse hair shone refulgent on his glittering casque, which concealed his still brighter eye.

With a savage and disdainful look, Edmund surveyed his youthful antagonist; who, conscious of having received an unmerited insult, was no less impassioned.

The trumpets sounded the charge, and their first encounter was so rude, they were both near losing their seats. Their second meeting was equally furious; their lances shivered in their hands, on which they dismounted, and drew their falchions, whose tempered blades, from the dexterity with which they were wielded, cast a dread gleam on the spectator's eyes. Long they fought with a courage almost supernatural, till a well aimed blow from the sword of Leonard, cleft Fitzallan's orbed shield in twain; but scorning to take an advantage, he instantly disengaged himself from his own. The combat was then continued with greater vigour, if possible, than before: the sweat, the dust and gore, flowed down their aching limbs. Leonard, at length, wearied with the combat, sunk on his knee; on which his adversary rushed furiously at him, but the youth nimbly recovered his legs, and avoided the blow; while Edmund missing his intended object, fell prostrate on the earth.

The shouts of the populace rent the air; but the generous victor, nothing elated by the acclamations bestowed upon him, assisted his enemy to rise, and considering him no longer so, assured him, the dispute which had taken place between them on the preceding evening, was on his part totally forgotten.

Edmund received his courtesy with a coolness, which even his dissimulation could not conceal, and retired thoroughly chagrin'd, and within himself vowing vengeance, for having been thus vanquished by a stripling.

So true is it that the offender, far from burying past quarrels in oblivion, generally keeps a jealous eye upon the noble object he has insulted.

"Forgiveness to the injured does belong,
They seldom pardon that have done the wrong."

The Lord De Courci, his Lady, and every one present, congratulated Leonard on his conquest; while he, so far from being vain of the compliments he received, seemed abashed at those commendations that were justly his due.

His wounds growing cold, became so painful, they compelled him to retire to his couch, which he kept for several days; and during that time his host's family endeavoured to render his confinement as little irksome as possible, by being frequently in his company. Gertrude, the consort of De Courci, was particularly attentive, more, indeed, than became her situation; she was oft in his apartment, and her eyes told him the inward workings of her heart; she would sit and gaze upon his countenance, while sigh would echo sigh!

The faithful Owen, who had been an anxious spectator of the combat, and had thrown himself on his knees, to return thanks to heaven for Leonard's victory, the instant it was over, scarce ever quitted the chamber during his illness, and sought, by his wit and humour, to cheer the drooping spirits of his master.

In the course of conversation 'twixt the Knight and his 'Squire, the quarrel of the latter with Stephen was brought forward on the carpet. Leonard had received an indistinct relation of the tale, and therefore embraced the present leisure opportunity of making himself acquainted with the real circumstances of it. Owen related the greater part of the story truly and honestly: the principal event, however, which had occurred, respecting the discharge of the log at his antagonist's head, was totally obliterated; for, as the story stood on the record of his own fancy, himself gave the first challenge; drew the first sword; made the first attack; forced the first blood; and, first and lastly, felled poor Stephen insensate to bite his mother earth.

Leonard's youth, and a good constitution, soon restored him; on which, his first inquiry was after Edmund, who, they informed him, was conveyed from the castle in a litter, immediately after the tournament.

His health being re-established, he frequently took the exercise of riding, in order to recruit his strength: returning one evening, later than usual, he was beset by four ruffians, who, without receiving, or assigning any cause, attacked him. He did every thing possible for a man in his situation, and defended himself with the bravery of an hero; but was so weakened by his late illness, he must inevitably have fallen a sacrifice, had not the noble Edgar, like his guardian angel, arrived at the very moment one of the villains, with a battle-axe, had felled him from his horse.

Young De Courci, who finding his friend did not return at the accustomed time, was come in quest of him, without reflecting on the odds he had to encounter, attacked the bravadoes, and quickly laid two dead at his horse's hoofs; and in the mean while, Leonard recovering, the others took to flight.

The young Knight could scarce express his gratitude, "Accept," said he, "my warmest, my sincerest thanks: but for your timely aid, I had, 'ere this, been numbered with the dead. It seems, my destiny is to increase the obligations I owe your noble family, and which my humble state forbids me the hope of ever repaying. Believe me, I cannot play the orator, but when the sense of your generosity is effaced from my memory, then must the vital springs of life cease to animate my clay."

They returned to the castle, conversing on the subject of this strange adventure: neither could conceive why men, thus unprovoked, should attack a fellow-creature: plunder was not their drift, but blood.

De Courci and his lady were rejoiced at Leonard's arrival; but when he made them acquainted with the miraculous escape he had experienced, through the valour of their noble son, their happiness was redoubled: even Gertrude relaxed her usual severity of features towards Edgar, and applauded his conduct, while the unfeigned tear of joy trickled down the cheek of Owen, on hearing how providentially his master had escaped the swords of the assassins.

"Ah, sir!" said he, "I would I had been with you."

"You," replied Leonard, "Why will you fight?"

"I cannot tell," said the 'Squire, "I never tried; but had I seen you in danger, I would have laid about me with the best of them. By the valour of my ancestors! I should have been as bold as *Beauchamp!*"

"Thou art a good fellow," returned the Knight, "take this piece of money."

"No, my Lord," exclaimed Owen, "believe me, I would rather possess your good opinion than your gold."

Then bowing, he retired to the kitchen, where he protested, there was not such a Knight living as the one he served, nor such a 'Squire as himself.

About this time letters arrived from Edward, summoning De Courci and his vassals, to join him immediately. The Baron thought he had done his part in the service of his country, and resolved to spend the autumn of his years in calm retirement: he resigned therefore the command of his troops to his son and Leonard.

The latter, having been some time absent from his native fields, became anxious once more to see his parents: nor was Emma the least powerful magnet that attracted his thoughts to Northumberland. He informed his noble host, that he must, though reluctantly, take his leave of him, as duty and affection required his attendance on the authors of his being, 'ere he left England. The Baron, sorry to be deprived of so agreeable a guest, yet esteemed him more than ever for his filial piety.

CHAPTER VI

——Ha! who comes here?
I think it is the weakness of mine eyes,
That shapes this monstrous apparition—
It comes upon me—Art thou any thing?
Art thou some God, some Angel, or some devil,
That mak'st my blood cold, and my hair to stare?

THE morn arriving, on which they were to quit the friendly walls of Lord De Courci's mansion, they were about to depart, when intelligence was brought, that Owen was no where to be found. Every avenue of the gothic fabric was searched, but to no purpose. At length, in the height of his vexation, Leonard determined to tarry no longer; but to set forward without him, when the 'Squire appeared, pacing towards the castle, with a slow and dismal step. On his near approach, his master observed his eyes were suffused with tears, and inquiring into the cause, was informed he had been to take leave of his aged parents, who, he said, were much distressed. "I am going," he continued, "where many a better fellow than myself has been made shorter by the head, and, as I am not at present above the middle size, I cannot conceive my figure would be improved by the loss."

Here Leonard interrupted him, and putting a purse of gold into his hand, said, "Go, give this to your venerable parents; tell them to be of comfort, and do you rouze all that is man within you. Remember, the same Omnipotent Being, who rescued me from the merciless swords of the assassins, will bear a shield before you in the day of battle!"

"I hope," replied his follower, "it will be a seven-fold one! though, to say truth, I do not think I shall have much occasion for it, as I have already procured the largest I could find in the armoury."

"Peace," cried his master, "away, and hasten your return."

The grateful fellow ran swiftly to the cottage of his youth, and was soon back again. They then took leave of the Lord De Courci, who, with the Baroness, crossed the drawbridge, and followed them with his eyes, till distance obscured them from their sight: they then re-entered the castle, lamenting their loss.

It is now proper to advert to Emma, who, during the absence of her lover, had pined in melancholy. The rose, that once bloomed upon her cheek, gave way to the pallid hue of the lily; her herds were neglected: no strain of harmony could she draw from her late favourite lute; she forsook the vale for the melancholy shade of the encircling grove, in which she chiefly passed her time. There she was sitting, attentive to the moan of the turtle dove, and commenting upon their constancy, when the blast of a distant trumpet saluted her ear. She arose, and ran to the margin of the wood; from the opposite side she saw a large troop of horsemen enter the dale, and proceed to the castle. She then retraced her steps into the leafy labyrinth, her thoughts wholly occupied with the idea of her loved Leonard. She doubted his constancy: she had received no letter from him since his departure: the sight of the warriors revived her anxiety, and she abandoned herself to all the agony of grief.

In the interim the troops, who were those of De Courci, entered the castle, and the son of that Baron delivered his letters from Fitzallan to the steward. Leonard embraced the first opportunity of visiting his father and mother, in which he was accompanied by Edgar. Their joy at meeting being somewhat allayed, their son presented his friend.

"Behold," he said, "the man to whose family I stand indebted for all I now enjoy. Oh! teach me, my beloved parents, how to repay the obligation!"

"I thank heaven," exclaimed Christopher, "that has raised you up such powerful friends: nor am I less grateful, that it has endowed you with a mind to retain the sense of what you owe them! Continue your glorious course."

"Ah!" cried Barbara, "your head runs upon nothing but battles. Do not return to the wars, Leonard, you are rich enough now, and may live at ease!"

"Silence," replied Christopher, with a frown, "a pretty lesson you would inculcate. What! when his King has re-warded him with riches, and honours, would you have him desert the cause by which he gained them? By heaven! I would sooner see him dead at my feet, than guilty of such meanness!"

"Fear not my conduct," said the youth, "I trust the precepts you instilled into my breast, will never be eradicated."

"I fear it not," returned his father, "but this good woman vexes me: she had better stick to her distaff than meddle with these affairs."

Leonard then inquired after Emma, and how it was she did not answer his letters; at which the old people betrayed evident marks of confusion. Again he interrogated them, but received no answer. Shook by suspense, he left the cottage, and flew to that of his loved mistress, where he was informed by her mother she was not within. "Since your departure," continued she, "I know not what has ailed the girl: she passes most of her time in the wood, nor scarce ever returns till sun-set."

Leonard tarried to hear no more, but rushed in quest of her, and had not penetrated far into the grove, 'ere his progress was stopped by the well-known voice of Emma, who was singing the following:

> The swelling sails now catch the breeze;
>   The pilot at the helm does stand;
> The bark impetuous ploughs the seas,
>   And sailors wishful eye the land.

So by the breath of sour mischance,
     My bosom's driven by the gale;
While sigh on sigh resembles zephyr,
     And my shatter'd spirits fail.

The faint moon my hopes resemble,
     When thro' clouds she's seen in part;
Her beams that on the waters tremble,
     Picture well my flutt'ring heart.

O may kindly winds befriend me;
     Waft Leonard to his native shore:
Adversity then will not bend me,
     For then can grief return no more.

He listened with attention, and caught each syllable; then gently crept through the impervious shade, and beheld the maiden seated on an eminence, with her eyes fixed on the billows that flowed beneath. Like a mournful willow, she bent her body over the waves, and sighed, while the soft breezes bore them up to heaven, and recording angels registered them in the leaves of maiden constancy. So wholly was she absorbed in reverie, she did not perceive her lover's approach, till his embrace caused her to start: but on discovering who it was, her fear was converted into joy.

"My dear loved Emma!" exclaimed Leonard, "forgive my intruding thus upon your solitude; but my wish to see you could not be restrained. How have I languished for this joyful meeting! Amidst the clangour of the war, you were the constant inmate of my heart, and led me on to glory."

"No doubt," said the maid, "I must have engrossed your thoughts in the hour of danger, when even in peace you could not find a leisure minute to send me one consolatory line."

"What means my life?" replied he, "Each billet that I sent my parents was accompanied by one for you. Is it possible you did not receive them?"

"Never!" returned Emma, "and I began to fear the splendid dames who attend the court, had lured your heart from me."

"Impossible!" cried Leonard, "true as the needle to its northern pole, will ever be my love. Still I cannot but blame my parents for not delivering my letters to you. Had they ever known the pangs of absent lovers, they would have acted otherwise."

His cheeks, at these words, were flushed with rage.

"Think no more of it," quoth Emma, "convinced of your tenderness, all former sorrows are lost in the pleasure of this blessed interview."

They then renewed their vows of constancy, and that, nor time nor chance should ever have power to shake it: that, indeed, was impossible, their hearts were too firmly united by the chains of affection, forged on the anvil of sacred virtue!

He conducted Emma home, and then repaired to the castle, where a magnificent banquet was provided. Mirth presided at the social board, and every unpleasing thought was buried in oblivion, or drowned in the mantling bowl. They then separated, and Leonard was conducted to an apartment that bore the marks of ancient grandeur, but which appeared much out of repair. The furniture was quite decayed; the tapestry dropping from off its hangings, and the rich green velvet curtains that adorned the bed, were all in shreds, while the deep gold fringe was turned to a copper colour.

The Knight could not refrain from moralizing on the scene. "Such," said he to himself, "such is the state of man: when in prosperity, the world pays homage to him, but if distress or age e'er dims his lustre, like swallows at the approach of winter, they take their leave: so is it by this chamber; no doubt but it was once the cause of admiration, though now neglected."

He seated himself before the fire, and drew out the miniature which Christopher had given him on his first quitting his native cottage. Intelligence sparkled in the countenance of the portrait, though dimmed by a pensive melancholy, which the artist seemed to have designed, to give the features greater interest;—nor did he think of retiring, till the castle clock announced the hour of one in deep strains, which rolled through the various avenues of the edifice, and filled the mind of Leonard with a thrilling melancholy. He arose from his seat, with a determination to adjourn to his couch, when he perceived a part of the tapestry shake in a violent manner: he approached, and lifting up the hanging, to his surprise, discovered a small door, which he endeavoured to open, but was much mortified on finding it was fast locked. For a long time he vainly strove to force it: at length he succeeded, but was almost petrified, when he discovered, in a small apartment, a doublet all besmeared with blood, and a sword dyed in the same purple stream. "Gracious powers," he involuntarily exclaimed, "What can this mean?" While he, fascinated, gazed upon the bloody spectacle before him, a rustling in the apartment he had just quitted, aroused him from the stupefaction wherein horror had plunged him, and turning his head, he beheld a figure, compleatly armed, on which he rushed into the room, but could discover no one.

He examined minutely the hangings, but could find no clue to guide him: he tried the outer door, which was fast, as he had left it.

Horror-struck, he knew not which way to turn his eyes, or how to act, till reposing his trust in the Omnipotent Being, and offering up his prayers to heaven, the passive stream of reason flowed over his ruffled mind, and calmed his stormy spirits. He cheered his fire, and placing his falchion by him on the table, passed the remainder of the night undisturbed.

CHAPTER VII

Of battles bravely, hardly fought: of victories
For which the conqueror mourn'd, so many fell:
— — — — — — — — —
Now all the youth of England are in arms,
And silken dalliance in the wardrobe lies:
Now strive the armourers and honours thought
Reigns solely in the breast of every man:
They fell the pasture now to buy the horse,
Following the mirror of all Christian Kings,
With winged heels, as English Mercuries.

SHAKESPEARE.

AFTER a sleepless night, Leonard arose, and, opening the window, was surprised to find himself, from the situation, in that very apartment, asserted to be the haunt of some disembodied spirit. Although his understanding was too enlightened to give credit unto so idle a tale, yet, the occurrences he had met with, somewhat shook his incredulity, and he immediately repaired to the cottage of his father, where he imparted all that had happened.

Christopher shook his head: Barbara sighed, and seemed about to answer, but was checked by a frown from her husband, who then addressed his son.

"Leonard," he said, "if you value your own safety, or our peace, reveal to no one what you saw last night; keep the secret to yourself: heaven will, in its own good time, discover all."

The manner in which these words were uttered, though they convinced the youth there was some mystery attending the castle, with which his parents were not wholly unacquainted, prevented his putting any farther interrogatory; nor, during his stay in the valley, did he ever renew the subject.

The period fixed for the Knight's departure, at length arrived, and he once more abandoned this peaceful spot, to

40

encounter the dangers of the war, of which the following was the cause.

Edward had received intimation, that the gallic monarch had equiped a vast armament by sea and land, and had invested David Bruce, the Scottish King, with the command of his navy, who scoured the English channel, while a strong army threatened to invade Guienne.

The Sovereign of England, though he wished to avoid an open rupture with France, sent for a fleet from Bayonne, to oppose his enemies: and though he could not put a stop to the preparations that were making in Denmark, Norway, and Holland, yet his interest prevailed in Genoa and Provence, who refused Philip de Valois the aid he had craved for the feigned purpose of a crusade. He, at the same time, granted a commission to Geoffrey de Say, to raise a squadron, and assert his dominion on the sea, whose sceptre had ever been in the possession of his ancestors, and the influence of which he determined should not diminish under his sway.

He had made attempts to compromise his difference with the French King; but now, seeing through the affected delays of his opponent, he would be no longer trifled with, and instantly prepared for war: to effect which, he deemed it politic to strengthen himself by foreign alliances, and therefore empowered his allies on the continent, to enter into league with such Princes as they thought might prove beneficial to the cause; and, being thus unwillingly involved in a war, resolved not only to strive for the recovery of his lands in Guienne, but, for the whole kingdom of France, to which he considered himself rightful heir, as nearest in consanguinity to the late King.

These sentiments were encouraged by Robert D'Artois, at that time a refugee in England: he had married a sister of Philip's, and, presuming on the alliance, revived a law-suit for the recovery of Artois, which had formerly been adjudged in favour of his aunt Maud; and, in order to support his claim, produced several deeds, forged for the occasion: but, the counterfeit being detected, the author, (a lady of Bethune) in consequence of her own confession, was condemned to the stake, and Robert dismissed from the court.

Being afterwards summoned by his Peers, to answer for this subornation, he refused to appear; on which account his estates were confiscated, himself banished, and he retired to England, where he was entertained by Edward, with the same munificence that David Bruce experienced in France. Being possessed of an uncommon share of courage and capacity, he soon made himself conspicuous in council, while his inveterate hatred to Philip ever prompted him to declare for war.

The King, however, who was not actuated by the same motives, agreed to leave his dispute, relative to Guienne, unto the decision of the Pope, who exhorted the Gallic Monarch to do him justice, that, peace being restored, he might bear the blessed cross against the infidels. This remonstrance, nevertheless, was productive of nought but evasive answers; on which the Pontiff pressed him either to commence the voyage, or refund the money which had been raised by the Clergy towards the charges of the expedition; and Philip, who could no longer amuse his Holiness with vague promises, declared he never would be on terms of amity with Edward, until David Bruce was restored to the throne of Scotland, and D'Artois driven from the English court.

To the first, the King of England declared, he would sooner extirpate the whole race of Caledonians, than assent to so unreasonable a demand: to the latter, he replied, his honour had been given to protect Robert, and, however lightly his brother Philip might consider that pledge, he held it sacred; nor would he derogate from his own dignity so far, as to drive an exile from the asylum he had once promised him.

Every thing now foretold an approaching war: the French commenced hostilities, by seizing the castles of the province of Guienne, and Edward called a parliament, wherein he disclosed his cause of quarrel; the vain steps he had taken towards an accommodation, and the progress he had made in his foreign alliances. The Senate, as well as the nation in general, applauded the conduct of their Prince, and burnt with generous ardour to engage his foes, who had thus, unprovoked, waged war against him.

The Bishop of Lincoln, with the Earls of Salisbury and Huntingdon, were appointed Commissioners to finish the treaties with the several potentates; and arriving at the court of Hainault, with a large retinue of Barons and Knights, they entered into league with that Count, the Duke of Brabant, the Marquis of Juliers, and various other Princes. They endeavoured to attach Lewis, the Count of Flanders, to their interest, by proposing a marriage between his son, and the King's daughter; but so intimately was he connected with Philip, that the temptation failed. This, however, did not prevent their tampering with the Flemings, who were particularly inimical to the French, and had every reason to favour Edward, on account of the considerable advantages they derived from their commerce with England. Some of the large towns were, in a manner, independant of the Count, and were, in reality, governed by a wealthy brewer, named Jacob Van Ardevelt. This man was of a most enterprizing disposition, and, though a plebeian, possessed such immense riches, that he maintained a guard of eighty soldiers about his person, and kept spies all over the country: he was more absolute than the Count himself; employed emissaries to dispatch some noblemen, and banished others who had the temerity to oppose his injustice. In short, he was one of those subjects a Prince ought to ruin, or keep fair with; and this man did the Bishop of Lincoln undertake to win to the English cause; as also the cities of Bruges and Ypres; in all which he succeeded.

On the other side, Count Lewis espoused the interest of Philip, with such a degree of enthusiasm, that, without form of trial, he put a nobleman of Courtnay to death, merely because he was suspected to be a favourer of Edward: he also sent Guy de Rockenbourg, with a power to take possession of the Isle of Dadsant; and as, by these means, he was enabled to cut off all communication by sea to Ghent or Bruges, the English Sovereign dispatched the Earls of Suffolk and Derby, as the head of four thousand men, to dislodge them. The place, however, was obstinately defended; in spite of which, the English, bearing down all opposition, made good their footing on the beach, when a fierce engagement ensued, in which the enemy were routed, three thousand slain upon the spot, and their leader captured, whose ransom fell to Sir Walter Manny, a Knight of great prowess, and who had, during the combat, saved the life of Lord Derby.

Ardevelt, who warmly supported the cause of Edward, instantly entreated him to come over, and head the allies in person, which, however, he thought prudent to decline for the present, as the Count of Hainault was dead: and, though his son declared for England, yet the cause found so heavy a loss in the father, that it seemed as a limb lopped from the body of their enterprize. He therefore appointed John, Duke of Brabant, his Lieutenant in France; and, moreover, authorized him to take possession of that kingdom. But, as war was not yet declared, the Pontiff of Rome strained every nerve to avert those woes and calamities, which he saw must inevitably attend a contest between Princes so powerful; and prevailed on Edward to name commissioners to negotiate a peace with the nations of France and Scotland. Two Cardinals were sent over to interpose their good offices, and a suspension of arms was agreed on till the subsequent year.

Mean-while, Edward convened his Parliament, who granted him an enormous subsidy, which, notwithstanding, was inadequate to the expences of his armament and treaties of alliance; for the German Princes were ever as insatiate, and exorbitant in their demands, as they were backward in making good their agreements. The King, at this period, having prevailed on several potentates of Gascony to renounce all fealty to

Philip; and, having borrowed money of the different abbeys, embarked forthwith at Orewell, (where he was joined by Leonard and Edgar) with a numerous fleet and army, and, landed at Antwerp, the capital of his ally, John of Brabant.

On the day following, he held a conference with Ardevelt, who advised him to assume the title of King of France, which would serve as an excuse to the Flemings for taking up arms against their Lord.

Edward, who had long wavered on this subject, was easily persuaded to adopt a measure he was before half inclined to follow. He had dispatched ambassadors to treat for a peace with Philip, whom he then stiled Sovereign of Gallia; but he now prohibited their doing ought that might be prejudicial to his own claim, or termed an acknowledgement of his opponent's title. As for the homage he had formerly paid that Prince, at Amiens, he avowed it to be the act of a minor, extorted from him, and concluded by proclaiming Philip an usurper.

A convention of the allies was now held, at which all were present, save the Duke of Brabant, whose absence served as a pretext for the rest not affording their aid, until he should act in concert with them.

Leonard, whose passion broke down the barrier of reason on all occasions, and whose affection for his sovereign now prompted him, bitterly upbraided them, adding, the Duke's non-attendance was but a shallow pretence for their not fulfilling their engagements, and boldly told them, such Princes as themselves, whom neither faith or honour could bind, were unfit to govern. Edgar endeavoured to restrain his ire, well knowing they could fully revenge themselves by the base means of assassination; but nought could prevent his uttering the dictates of his heart, and he continued his reproaches, until the commands of the King bridled his tongue.

Edward now found the imprudence of which he had been guilty, in confiding so implicitly on their protestations; but, as he had gone too far to retract, with honour, he used every means his invention could devise, to prevail on the Duke of Brabant to enter cordially into his views; and so effectually did his purpose answer, that John, although he had solemnly assured Philip he never would bear arms against him, yet, won by promises, he gave his word to renounce all connexion with that Prince, and to assist the allies to the utmost of his power.

Upon this they agreed to attack France forthwith, provided they could obtain permission of the Imperial crown, to which they were subject, and this they hoped easily to gain, as the King of France had encroached upon the empire, by taking the castle of Crevecœur, and putting a garrison into Cambray.

Edward, therefore, dispatched the Marquis of Juliers to Coblentz, and shortly after repaired thither himself, where the Emperor readily granted all he asked, and, moreover, created him Vicar of the empire, an office which gave him absolute authority over his German allies. After a short sojourn at this court, he returned to Brabant, where he thought it prudent to spend the winter, that, being at hand, he might quicken the preparations, and at the same time intimidate the Bishop of Liege, whom he knew to be strongly in Philip's interest: on this account he sent for his Queen Philippa to Antwerp, where she was delivered of her third son, Lionel, afterwards Duke of Clarence.

Edward's alliance with Lewis of Bavaria, greatly offended the Pope, who had pronounced the sentence of excommunication against him, for setting up an anti-pope, and the King of England was exhorted to break all connexion with him, on peril of the same censure: he, however, paid no regard to the idle threats of a Pontiff, whom he knew ever to have been his foe, and, careless of the consequence, prepared for a vigorous war.

Having compleated his forces, he marched into the Cambresis, and reduced the castles thereof: from thence he proceeded to the Vandermois; and though the Counts of Hainault and Namur abandoned him on his first entering that country, he resolved to besiege Cambray, and actually encamped before it;

but finding the place too well supplied with men, and provision, for him to entertain a hope of reducing it, either by force or famine, he abandoned the project, and marched towards Peronne, where the army of Philip lay, whom he desired to appoint a day for battle. At the time fixed, both armies drew up in array, and remained facing each other, till darkness overshadowing the earth, they retired.

"Ha sir!" said Owen, (who accompanied his master) when they entered the tent of the latter, "I would every day might end as peaceably as this has done; and, let me tell you, there would be sound policy in so doing, for if there was no fighting, there would be twice as many soldiers as there are at present! truly, these Frenchmen, though they are our enemies, seem very quiet people, and, was I compelled to the alternative, I would rather encounter five of those gentlemen, than one of those brawny Scotch devils I have heard so much about. *By the valour of my ancestors!* the sight of their *cut* and *thrusts* must be enough to make a coward tremble; and, I am told, they make no more of chopping a poor fellow's head in two, than I should of twisting a capon's neck!"

"Well," quoth Leonard, "to-morrow the army will be again drawn out, and I sincerely wish you may have an opportunity of encountering these sons of Gallia: at the same time, let me caution you not to think too lightly of them, or you may find, to your cost, the folly of your conjecture."

Owen's spirits were reduced by this account, and he thought the surest, and pleasantest means of recruiting them, would be a flaggon of wine: the idea was immediately adopted, and to every cup he drank a *speedy peace, and a safe return to Old England.*

CHAPTER VIII

——Some strange commotion
Is in his brain; he bites his lip and starts;
Stops on a sudden, looks upon the ground,
Then lays his finger on his temple; strait,
Springs out into fast gait, then stops again;
Strikes his breast hard, and then, anon he casts
His eye against the moon: in most strange postures
We've seen him set himself.

SHAKESPEARE.

BY early dawn, the armies were again drawn out in battle-array, and so continued till noon, when the French retreated to their quarters, which they fortified with trenches, and trunks of trees, while the English marched towards Avesnes, and Edward sent a defiance to Philip, conjuring him to spare the lives of so many, and to decide their dispute by single combat, engaging to resign all pretensions to France, should he be vanquished.

The Gallic Monarch was much disposed to accept the challenge, but his Barons set forth the imprudence of risking his crown with an enemy, whom the weather would, in a short time, compel to leave the field. His answer was, "That he should not stoop so much beneath his own dignity, as to put himself on a footing with his vassal, whom he would chastise in a manner more accordant with his insolence and perfidy."

On this he retired to Paris, and Edward returned to Brussels.

Among the subjects of Philip, none distinguished themselves so eminently as the Normans, who sent deputies to their Sovereign, with an offer to invade England, provided he would put his eldest son, John, at their head, whom they proposed to place upon the throne of Albion; and moreover undertook to furnish him with four thousand men at arms, ten thousand bow-men, and three times that number of infantry. Their design however proved abortive, through the vigilance of Edward's navy, commanded by Lord Morely, who destroyed a great part of their fleet, and levelled Treport to the ground.

The King of England expended immense sums in his first campaign, in lieu of which he had gained no solid advantage, and now found himself in great difficulties for want of money: he therefore sent over to England the state of his necessities, and to demand a subsidy. The parliament met, but some disputes taking place, relative to the business, it was postponed, which much enraged Edward, as the allies were now grown clamorous, and John of Brabant would not permit him to visit his own country, till he had given security for his return. This Prince he presented with a great annuity, and promised the Marquis of Juliers an English Earldom. He had made several attempts to draw the Count of Flanders from Philip, but all in vain; and seeing now no prospect of a reconciliation, he quartered the arms of France with England: the inscription of the great seal was altered from *Duke of Aquitain,* to *King of France:* the former motto was erased, and that of *Dieu et mon Droit* substituted; alluding to the justness of his cause, and of his fixed resolve to support the title he had assumed.

A treaty was then concluded between Edward and the Flemings, who still remained firm to him, and, in a consultation with the allies, it being agreed to open the campaign with the siege of Tournay, he quitted the continent, and landed at Harwich.

The carnage of war being now ended, Leonard and Edgar, with that curiosity so natural to youthful minds, resolved to visit the Pyrenean mountains, whose tops ascend to heaven; and, attended by their 'Squires, bent their course towards those famous hills. One evening, as they pursued their journey, a lady passed them at full speed on horseback, followed by a man, who watched, with anxiety, the swiftness with which the female's courser bore her. De Courci immediately clapping spurs to his steed, pursued their track: Leonard was about to imitate his example, when the dismal howl of a wolf arrested his purpose, and he halted to assail the ferocious animal, whose eye-balls strained by rage and hunger, darted a fiery gleam around. The Knight, however, nothing daunted, waited his attack, and dyed his tempered falchion in the purple stream of life; when, with a roar that echoed through the forest, the savage monster ploughed the earth with his keen teeth, and died.

Owen, whose fright had deprived him of speech, now that he saw this formidable enemy breathless, exhorted his master to make off with as much speed as he could, adding, he had heard wolves made their excursions in as large bodies as the French soldiers; and though they had escaped one, it was not very probable they should be able to vanquish a whole army.

Leonard paid little attention to this salutary observation, but rode forward in quest of his companion. Having followed the same route for several leagues, the darkness of the night banished the hope of overtaking him, and he alighted at the first house they reached, where he tarried till break of day, and again resumed his journey; but no track or tidings could he gain of his lost friend: he repeated his inquiry at every place through which they passed, but all to no effect; nor had he collected any intelligence of Edgar, when the gigantic summit of the Pyrenees, whitened by the pale snow of heaven, struck their sight. Drawing near, Leonard took his course along the base of one of those towering mountains, and beheld a man suddenly dart from behind a grassy bank, and ascend the rugged hill with the swiftness of the antelope.

Leonard had time to gain only a partial view, by which he discovered him to be nearly without vestment: as he remained following the fugitive with his eyes, he was struck by a voice, which in an impassioned tone, pronounced, "Poor soul!"

This exclamation drew his attention, and, turning round, he descried an aged shepherd, gazing also at the object who had excited his surprise, while the drop of pity moistened his beard. The Knight, imagining from his behaviour, he could give some account of him who fled, accosted him.

"You seem, my good old friend," said he, "to speak with feeling: know you the person to whom, I conceive, your words alluded?"

"Do you mean," returned the peasant, "that unfortunate being who just now passed you?"

"I do," quoth Leonard, "and, from the compassion with which your speech was uttered, I imagine you are interested for him; perhaps allied to him?"

"Indeed, sir," replied the rustic, "I am no way related to him, save that we all derive our existence from Adam: his sufferings command my pity, and I feel as much for him as though he were my brother! Good heaven! what had that poor creature endured? twenty years has he passed upon these bleak mountains, without raiment to preserve his limbs from the cold, or an habitation to shelter him from the inclemency of the weather. Sorry fare for so long a period!"

"Indeed," cried the son of Christopher, "so long?"

"Aye," said the shepherd, "it is so indeed! no one knows from whence he came, for he will not hold converse with any body: at times you may hear him sing different ditties, which make the neighbours suppose he has been crossed in love; but, in the midst of them, he will suddenly break off, start from the rock whereon he hath seated himself, turn his eyes to heaven, clasp his hands in agony, then, casting a look around, as though he were fearful some one saw him, whom he wished to avoid, dart up the hill even as you saw him now."

Leonard found his curiosity greatly excited by this recital, and determined, if possible, to draw the recluse into discourse. He possessed a vast share of the milk of human kindness: philanthropy was an inmate of his heart; and to relieve his fellow-creatures, was the greatest happiness he knew. The calls of nature, however, prevented his putting his scheme into immediate execution, and he inquired of the peasant whether there was any place near, at which he could gain some slight refreshment?"

"Why signior," said he, "I have nothing but milk and fruit; if you can make a meal of them, you are welcome."

Leonard gladly embraced the offer, and accompanied him to a small hut, where the coarse fare was produced; and though the mind of the Knight was much too occupied to admit his regaling heartily, yet Owen, whose softer feelings ever gave way to the cries of hunger, made a more vigorous attack on the provisions, than he ever had done upon the enemy.

Their repast ended, the son of Christopher named his intention to his host, who agreed to accompany him up the mountain. Owen would fain have excused himself from being of the party; having satisfied his appetite, he now wished for a little repose, and would have preferred a few hours slumber to all the enterprizes the whole race of Knights-errant ever undertook.

He was forced, nevertheless, to accompany Leonard, and quitted the cottage very reluctantly. As they ascended, his natural good humour returned, and the stupendous heights, that saluted his sight, called to recollection the Welch hills he had heard his father mention, who was indeed a native of that country, and he imparted these thoughts to his master.

"This place, sir," said he, "reminds me of the principality of my ancestors. Perhaps in such a spot was my great grandfather, Lewellyn, driven by his enemies."

"Lewellyn your great grand-father!" cried Leonard, supposing the poor fellow's brain was deranged.

"Yes," replied Owen; "my mother's father was natural son to that Prince; and, strange as it may appear, when persecuted by the English he swam across several rivers upon the roll of his pedigree! But pray, sir, do not walk quite so fast; nothing but a mule, or camel, could keep pace with you up this precipice: for my part, if I attempt it, I shall walk down again at one step, and then good-bye to our family, it will be extinct!"

They were now upon a part of the mountain, from whence, on one side, they beheld the plain they had just quitted; while, on the opposite, the ponderous rocks hung over them, and filled them with an apprehensive awe.

Suddenly the shepherd caught the arm of Leonard, and made a stop; at the same time pointing to a fragment, whereon was seated the object of their search. His left elbow was placed upon his knee, and on the same hand his cheek reclined; the other, encircling a large and knotted stick, pressed his heart, and, with a wildness, his looks were fixed upon the valley.

The young Knight had now leisure to contemplate his appearance accurately.

His head was silvered over with age, and a beard of the same fleecy hue, swept his broad and manly chest: the scythe of time had furrowed his countenance, as the plough leaves its traces on the face of earth: his eyes, though influenced by the same inveterate enemy to beauty, still retained a share of penetrating brightness: his form was majestic: no raiment had he on, save the covering of sheep-skin which fastened round his loins, descended half way down his legs: the upper part of him was bare, and totally unprotected against the seasons: in short, his whole appearance commanded pity and veneration.

The peasant now departed, and Leonard approached the recluse; who, observing him, was about to fly, when the youth suddenly halted, bowing at the same time with reverence; at which he made a pause, and, leaning on his massy stick, stared, with apparent wonder, at the Knight, who thus addressed him.

"Pardon what may seem an impertinent intrusion; if such you deem it, you will wrong me much: my only motive for breaking thus upon your solitude, is the hope of affording consolation to one, whom the malicious finger of fortune seems to have selected as a butt for her keenest arrows."

The stranger was silent: his eyes still bent on Leonard, who thus continued.

"I see my presence gives offence: yet, 'ere I depart, once more I conjure you to think more kindly of me, than that an idle wish to pry into your woes would lead me hither. Had my purse or sword the power to befriend you, they should be dedicated to your service: as it is, farewell! and may heaven administer that comfort, I fear man has not the ability to do."

As he spoke, the tears glistened in his eye, and, hiding his face beneath his hand, he was about to depart; but had measured only a few steps, 'ere the old man exclaimed, "It shall be so!" then turning to Leonard, "the accents of commiseration with which your words are uttered, and the proffer of your service, to a wretch unknown, demand alike my gratitude and wonder; and have caused me to break a vow made many years ago, that I would never henceforth hold converse with any human being. I return you my most fervent thanks; and the only proof I can give of the just sense I have of the obligation, is to entrust you with my history; though I fear the sufferings of an old man, with one foot already in the grave, will but fret the ear of a young Knight, like yourself, used, doubtless, to the gay pleasures of society."

Leonard assured him, that so far from the recital proving tedious, he should listen with pleasure, in the hope that his grief might find alleviation.

On this the stranger commenced his narrative.

54

CHAPTER IX

Oh, beware——of jealousy;
It is a green eyed monster, which doth make
The meat it feeds on.

SHAKESPEARE.

MY name is Hildebrand, England claims my birth; in the delightful county of ——, stands my paternal mansion, encircled
by fruitful woods and pastures. Blessed in a virtuous loving
consort, and a duteous son, my days glided by in happiness, nor
did aught seem wanting. Alas! how sadly reverse my present
state: the morning of my life basked in the sun-shine of felicity,
but the evening has been marked by crimes, and my night sets
in misery!

Bitter sighs, at these words, choaked the utterance of the
old man, while the stream of sorrow flowed down his cheek,
and grief sat pictured in his frenzied eye.

Pardon this digression, he cried, the remembrance of past
joys, though at the distance of many a long, long year, bears
down my reason, and drives me almost to a state of madness.

With rapture I beheld the increasing perfections of my son
Walter, and devoted my time in training his youthful mind to
trace the road of virtue. How amply were my cares rewarded!
even now, methinks, I view his countenance, beaming gratitude
and attention, as he listened to the documents his father laid
before him.

Thus did he spend his time, till he attained the age of manhood, when the fierce disputes between the ill-timed Edward
Caernarvon, and his Queen, spread civil war throughout the
nation. Whatever were the failings of that unhappy Monarch,
and many, I believe, they were, I resolved strictly to adhere in
my allegiance to him. From that period I date my woes.

About the same time, my son wished much to visit the
metropolis, to which I consented, and saw him quit the purlieus

of my castle with an aching heart. However, I shortly had the comfort of a letter, though not wholly unalloyed, as in it he highly extolled the Queen's favourite, Mortimer. Still I flattered myself it was nothing more than the temporary friendship of a raw youth; but when each billet teemed with fresh praises of the rebel, I began to suspect, by his arts, he had drawn my offspring from the duty he owed his Sovereign, and lowered him into a traitor.

On this, I instantly wrote to Walter, requesting his presence. His answer was filled with tenderness; he conjured me to dispense with his immediate attendance, as Mortimer was at that time making head against the Spenser's: that he had pledged himself to assist him with the vassals of his father, who he hoped would enable him to fulfil his promise.

Irritated at this declaration against his legal Monarch, I again summoned him, refusing either pecuniary, or any other aid, to a cause I despised.

With a manly, but submissive firmness, he replied, My anger was his only cause of sorrow: the sordid trash used by misers in their intercourse, and raked from the bowels of the earth, he contemned: the aid he had promised to his friend, he was prevented giving, but his single, arm, and sword, should be devoted to his service: and if he fell in battle, the only agonizing thought that would embitter his latest minutes, would be, that he died under the displeasure of a loved parent.

I wept over the paper that contained these lines, but my heart, of Adamantine hardness, forbade the entrance of the cherub meek-eyed pity; and I withstood the entreaties of my beloved Eleanor, who vainly pleaded for her offspring. Barbarian like, I persisted in my cruelty, and saw her reduced, by the ruthless fang of anguish, to a sick bed. There she had continued some time, when one morn, a gentle tap at my closet door arouzed me from a kind of lethargic meditation into which I had fallen: I opened it, and found it was the porter of the castle who had knocked.

"So, Hubert," said I, "what brings thee here?"

"Alas! my Lord," he cried, "I scarce know how to tell you: but you have been a kind master to me, and I cannot bear to see you injured, and sit tamely down as an accomplice."

His words excited my curiosity.

"Prythee cease your commendations," quoth I, "and impart your business."

"I will," he replied, "but restrain your anger, good sir, and, if possible, listen to me with calmness. Two nights ago, my lady's woman came to the gate, and informed me her mistress wished to speak with me.

"'With me,' returned I, 'Can'st tell what about?'

"'No,' retorted she, 'but you will learn that from herself.'

"I obeyed the summons and my lady thus accosted me.— 'Hubert,' she said, 'I think I can rely upon you; you are, I know, a faithful servant. Take this purse, and in return admit a stranger, who will knock gently at the gate about the hour of twelve: you will be near, and will conduct him hither, but, for your life, divulge not a syllable to my Lord!'

"I retired, having promised obedience to her commands; and, at the time mentioned, the person arrived, muffled in a horseman's coat, which effectually concealed his countenance. The female emissary was ready to receive him, and conducted him into the castle, where he remained for near two hours, then departed. This morning, Agnes once more accosted me, saying, 'Our visitor will be here again to night: be secret, and you are made for ever.'

"His intended coming a second time, struck me as suspicious, and I have revealed it to you, my Lord, that you may act as you think proper, and that I may have a load off my mind which troubles me."

I thanked my faithful domestick, continued Hildebrand, while every nerve in me was strained by jealousy and revenge. Thy fidelity, Hubert, I said, shall not go unrewarded. Admit this adulterer at the appointed time, and instantly repair to me; he shall be well provided for.

The porter retired, leaving me in a state painful, nay impossible, to describe. Impatiently I tarried the approach of night, and with rapture beheld the glittering car of Sol descend beneath the horizon, and the black pitchy mantle of darkness invade the earth, as most congenial with my feelings, and suited to my bloody purpose. The fatal hour at length arrived, and I heard footsteps softly creeping through the gallery. On opening the door, I found Hubert with a dark lanthorn, and, joining him, flew upon the sable wings of dire revenge to the apartment of my wife. I entered an adjacent closet, that commanded a prospect of the next room, and from thence saw a man, muffled in a cloak, his back towards me, and bent on one knee, pressing the hand of my wife to his lips, while she seemed to devour him with her eyes.

"Heaven knows," she cried, "how tenderly I love you, and how I have lamented the cruel chance that prevents me seeing you often!"

I could brook no more, but, overcome by jealousy and indignation, I rushed into the chamber, exclaiming, "Perfidious woman! be this the reward of thy boasted tenderness!" and, with these words, plunged my steel, even to the hilt, in the breast of the stranger, who staggered, groaned, and fell upon the couch, while Eleanor, with a loud shriek, threw herself upon him.

This, if possible, inflamed my temper more; I thought her lost to all decency, when even the presence of an injured husband could not restrain her lawless passion, and proceeded to drag her from the body. But what were my feelings at that moment? I tore her from the object, whereon she had cast herself, and the face of the man being now visible, presented to my astonished sight the features of my Walter! Pale, inanimate, distorted by the pangs of death!

What sufferings could equal mine? An only son weltering in gore, and deprived of existence by a murderous father: a wife, whose every wish consisted in my happiness, brought to the verge of the grave, and now a witness of her offspring's martyrdom. Grief, despair, every horrid passion, took possession of me: I wept, I raved, I cursed myself, and the hour in which I was created: but all in vain, my frenzy or repentance could not recall my son, whose death lays heavy on my head. Even now the recollection curdles my vital blood!

"The bare recital affects me exactly in the same manner," quoth Owen, who wished to return to the cottage, and satisfy his more predominant sense of tasting; "I think you had better finish your tale another time; your great men are always seeking food for the mind; now, for my part, I prefer a mutton cutlet, or a sirloin, to all the stories I ever heard."

Leonard silenced his loquacious 'Squire, and Hildebrand proceeded thus:

Frantick I quitted the castle, and, mounting my horse, made for the royal camp, hoping death would end my sufferings, and my guilt together. The soul-inspiring trumpet, on the subsequent morn, arouzed me; I quickly armed myself, and took my station, but neither the clangour of the war, nor the groans of wounded thousands, could divert my mind from a retrospection of my past crime. In every hostile helm methought the ghastly features of my murdered Walter darted reproach. I courted destruction, but to no purpose; the barbed arrows flew ineffectually round my wicked head, while they pierced the breasts of those, whose hearts were uncontaminated with vice.

The battle ended, and victory declared on our side, the shouts of conquering soldiers rent the air; each frame was actuated by excess of joy, save mine; which, callous to every sensation but despair, loathed even the sound of happiness. While the victors banquetted on their luxurious viands, I glutted upon melancholy, and, in this situation, remembrance presented these Pyrenean mountains: without delay I set off for them, and here have since sojourned. My food I gather, by the light of Cynthia, in the neighbouring vales:—the place suits well my distracted mind, for, when my pulse beats high, and heats my aged blood, I ascend the aspiring hills, and, in their snowy tops, seek to cool the raging stream of life; but, when the vital current slowly flows, or horror freezes every vein, from precipice to precipice I run and warm my icy body.

This is the history you desired to hear, and now, I pray you tell me, have I not cause to shun that world, which would revive my griefs, and in this dreary wild strive to atone my error?

Leonard acquiesced in what Hildebrand said; but at the same time used every argument to draw him from his retirement,

"Consider," cried the youth, "the rash act was not committed, supposing it was your son; and sure, the honour of an injured husband cannot be appeased, but by the blood of the adulterer. These were your sentiments at the fatal moment; and though you have to accuse fate that you have unwittingly shed your offspring's blood, yet sure your conscience may be easy."

"Excellent young man," exclaimed Hildebrand, "how few are like you! Oft have the passing populace ascended these steep hills to gaze at me, but never strove to sooth me with a word of comfort. Oft have they fixed their eyes upon my careworn form, while bursts of laughter shook their convulsed sides, and almost tempted me to cast their scoffing carcases from the stupendous height."

Here the fatigue of retrospection which his recital had harrowed up, much enfeebled him, and he ceased to speak, while night's black veil warned Leonard to retrace his steps down the precipice's side. After a sincere and friendly leave taking, he parted with the old man, and, returning to the cottage, passed the remainder of the evening in ruminating on the sufferings of Hildebrand, and the unfathomable ways of Providence!

CHAPTER X

He spoke, and high the forky trident hurl'd,
Rolls clouds on clouds, and stirs the watery world,
At once the face of earth and sea deforms,
Swells all the winds, and rouzes all the storms.
Down rush'd the night, east, west, together roar,
And south, and north, roll mountains to the shore.

POPE.

LEONARD shortly bade adieu to the Pyrenees, and bent his way towards ——, where he had the happiness to meet his friend Edgar, who gave him an account of the cause of their separation, in the following words.

You must remember the lady whose horse passed us with such velocity; I followed her for near a league, and, at length, had the mortification to see her unhorsed; on which I instantly dismounted, and ran to her assistance. Fortunately she had received no injury, for the ground whereon she fell was covered with a soft green turf. Just as she had recovered from the fright, wherein the accident had thrown her, an aged soldier joined us, and declared his joy on finding her unhurt.

Our care was now to find some habitation, where the lady might repose her for the night, and near at hand we espied a cottage: thither I conducted her, and knocked at the lowly portal, which was opened by a female, who granted the lodging we requested.

I then besought the fair stranger to inform me, by what cause I came to meet her almost unprotected?

She replied, to with-hold any intelligence from you, would be an ill requital for the service you have done me.

I am, by birth, an English woman, and was lately sent by my parents to pass a few months at the castle of the Count Saint Julian, not fifty leagues from hence: there I had been some time, when the son of that nobleman arrived, and, unfortunately,

61

fixed his affections on me. Having travelled most part of Europe, he had imbibed so vast a share of vanity, that he fondly imagined it impossible for any woman to look upon his person without admiring him. How it was, I know not, but I was blind to the perfections he possessed; and, when he condescended to reveal his passion, I entreated him to conquer it, as I had no thought of changing my estate.

He was much piqued at the careless manner in which I spoke, and told me there were several women, far my superiors, would have rejoiced at such a declaration; but advised me not to suppose he would easily give up the pursuit.

He then went immediately to his parents, to whom he related all that had passed, and I was soon after persecuted by their solicitations. But, on my firmly telling them I would never become the wife of the young Count, their rage knew no bounds, and they bitterly upbraided me; on which I declared my resolution to quit their mansion: this, they informed me, they would not consent to, and bade me despair of ever seeing my friends again, unless I gave my hand to their son.

I know not what I should have done, had not this faithful soldier, Oliver, whom my father had sent with me, effected my escape. He procured horses, and tarried for me at a small distance from the castle, from which place I walked, attended by an old woman, who watched me like my shadow. Oliver, however, spite of her cries, fastened her to a tree; then seating me on my steed, we proceeded towards the sea coast, and in our passage a wolf, who suddenly sprung at my courser, caused that noble creature to rush with violence from his sanguinary foe. I need say no more, than that I am much indebted to you, and never can I forget the obligation.

Thus ended she her narrative, quoth Edgar, on which I besought her to spare her acknowledgments, and to suffer me to be her safeguard wheresoever she might be going. She thanked me, and gave me permission to escort her to this port, which was the utmost I could obtain; and from hence she embarked, but where the vessel bore her I know not.

De Courci here paused, and the Knights, attended by their Squires, now quitted the continent, and embarked for their native country; but were scarce under way, when a violent storm overtook them: loud thunder shook the globe, and seemed as if it was again to be involved in ruin; darkness was spread over the surface of the deep, which was rendered more horrible by the forked lightning that gave a momentary flash, as though to shew the yesty waves, which, lion-mouthed, opened their ravenous jaws, and threatened instant death; while the wind fiercely whistled through the rigging, and chilled their very souls.

The tempest increasing, they were driven for several hours they knew not whither, and their bark, no longer obedient to the will of the mariners, struck upon a rock, and instantly parted. Being still dark, they could not receive any assistance from the inhabitants on shore, and most of the crew were lost. De Courci and Leonard, with Lewis, the follower of the former, by making themselves fast to a plank, gained the land at day break, and were soon observed by a fisherman, who was then going, the storm having somewhat subsided, to his vocation. His face, it is true, was not calculated to pre-possess the beholder in his favour, his features being far from regular, and his complexion of a comely copper. His heart, however, was actuated by compassion and generosity: he resembled a rough hewn casket, that at first we eye with indifference, but which, when we behold the jewel within, we treasure for the sake of what it contains.

Perceiving their situation, with humanity that would have done honour to one in an higher sphere, his only thought was about relieving them; he kindly, therefore, inquired if it was in his power to be of service to them? They thanked him, and asked the name of the place? He told them the Isle of Wight, and again offered his assistance.

I have, he said, a lowly, but I trust an hospitable cabin, the gang-way of which was never made fast against the entrance of the disabled, or the unfortunate. I have been a sailor, and, though for some time my voyages have been made only in my fishing smack, yet I have not so far forgot the character of a British seaman, as not to know his duty is to relieve the distressed. Hand me your yard-arms, and I will tow you into port in half a glass.

Without tarrying a reply, he took a hand of each, for they were very weak and exhausted, and led them to his cot, where they found the wife of their conductor, who, it is sufficient to say, possessed an heart like his own.

"Yo! ho! messmate," he exclaimed; "here are some strangers who have been ship-wrecked: I have pilotted them hither; and I trust you will give them the best cheer you can: Come, Ursula, let us sound your lockers! It is not low water, is it?"

Then having furnished them with fresh apparel, the homely fare, which consisted only of milk and dried fish, was spread upon the board, and the Knights eat with a better appetite than had they feasted on the choicest viands. Having ended their repast, they expressed a desire to discover some vessel that might convey them to England. This their host, whose name was Peter, undertook to procure, and strove, at the same time, to raise their drooping spirits.

"Come, your honours," he said, "never be down hearted; laugh at the storms of life: why I myself was beating up against the wind for several years, and have as many crosses on the log-book as any one. But, what then! why my timbers are of true English oak, and I buffeted the gale of sorrow, which made no more impression on my mind, than the wake of a ship leaves on the water." Then resigning his guests to the care of Ursula, he quitted the cottage.

The sun was just sunk beneath the western horizon; the faint recollection only of his rays still spangled the bosom of the old ocean, when the fisherman returned, accompanied by the unfortunate Owen, who, after testifying joy, and congratulating his master on their preservation, cried, "'Tis all mighty well, thank heaven, we have escaped drowning now, but do not let us tempt fate a second time, for the proverb may not be inclined to save us again. *By the valour of my Ancestors!* I would not undergo what I have lately done, to be restored to their possessions! First, to be thrown into a burning fever through fright, and then cast into the ocean, by way of a cold bath; and I too, that have as great an antipathy to water as a mad dog: at all events, I will not return home by sea, which is the most destructive, dangerous devilish——"

"Avast, you lubber!" exclaimed Peter, "ship a little manhood on board your crazy hulk, and swab the spray from your bows: why, d— me! they are as wet as if you had been turning to windward in a stiff gale! and harkee, my friend, though I am sorry for your mishap, and for any one that gets to leeward of fortune, yet you may chance to have a *salt eel* for your supper, if you offer to go to abuse the element by which I live, and by which, not only the wealth, but the glory, of old England is supported!—I beg pardon, your honours; I hope you will excuse the bluntness of an old weather-beaten tar; but I do not like to see a body put in their oar where they have no business. I have dispatches for you from our Baron, the Lord Montmorenci; bless his merry heart! he desires you will put in at his castle, where you will find better messing than in my poor birth."

"But how, my friend," said Leonard, "did he know we were your guests?"

"I told him," replied their host, "You must know I am a sort of a kind of a signal ship, stationed here upon the look-out; and, if I find any foundering on the shoals of distress, it is my post to hail our worthy Lord, who instantly lends them an hand. On parting company with you, I made sail for the castle, and informed him you had been shipwrecked, and that it was well you did not go to *Davy Jones;* on which he bade me steer you to him, where you will meet with good cheer I warrant. As I was homeward-bound, I fell in with this fair-weather spark, lying on the sands upon his back, poor fellow, like a turtle out of water: I poured a drop of grog down his throat, which set him afloat, and then convoyed him hither."

"Is the mansion of the Baron far from hence?" quoth Edgar.

"Far! Lord love your head," cried Peter, "why I can discern a sea-gull upon the battlements on a clear morning."

They then departed for the castle, and, arriving at the gate, dismissed their guide, to whom Leonard offered some pieces of money; "Take this," he said, "as a small recompence for your humanity."

"Begging your pardon," answered Peter, "it is no such thing; it is only the duty one fellow-creature owes another; and may he, who does not fully discharge that duty, never know the blessing of being himself assisted, or the satisfaction that accompanies a good action. Heaven bless your honours!"

Peter then turned his steps towards home, and the young Knights entered the courtyard; where, on their appearance, an aged man ran, and hailed the arrival of De Courci with every demonstration of joy; and Edgar immediately recognized the countenance of the faithful Oliver.

"My friend!" he exclaimed, "by what strange chance do I find thee here?"

"No matter, sir," replied the soldier, "there is one within, whose reception will give you more satisfaction than mine."

He then led them into a spacious apartment, where they were hospitably received by the Lord and mistress of the mansion; and soon after a young lady entered the room; but what were Edgar's sensations, when he discovered in her the fair one he had seen in France, escaping from her persecutors! Neither the Baron, his consort, or Leonard, could conceive the cause of their mutual surprise, till Julia, so was the female named, informed them that De Courci was the person who had so kindly and essentially served her while abroad.

The evening was passed in congratulatory conversation, and, on retiring, their slumbers were unbroken by the horrors of guilt, or the stings of a reproachful conscience. Such rest is ever sure to attend the pillows of the innocent!

During the evening, orders were given to take particular care of Lewis; as for Owen, he had kindly undertaken that hospitable office for himself; for, conscious of his being an utter stranger to this noble family, he had silently, and respectfully, retired from the presence of his master, on their first entering the castle; he soon, however, discovered the way of introducing himself into that quarter, where he could find a proper equality, and where he likewise made himself acquainted with the substantial means of regalement, after the fatigues of his voyage.

On rising in the morning, the warriors expressed their anxiety to depart, which their host strenuously opposed.

"No," he said, "I cannot consent so soon to lose you; and though the envious elements, against your inclinations, drove you hither, let me hope I shall owe your company, for a few days, to your own good will."

"We are much honoured by your invitation," replied De Courci, "but are expected by our friends. You, who are yourself a father, can well conceive the anxious care of a fond parent."

"I can," quoth the Baron, "and I thank heaven I can feel the power of gratitude! you befriended my child in a hard trying minute: the debt is by far too great ever to be cancelled, but let me at least endeavour to discharge a part of it: if my whole fortune could be considered as an equivalent, with pleasure I would resign it. Do not, I conjure you, refuse the only favour you can add to those we have already received. I will instantly dispatch messengers to your expectant families, provided you will give me their name and abode."

Edgar answered, "Your Lordship may command me; after what you have been pleased to say, I cannot but accept your proffered hospitality; and, since you generously offer to ease the raking doubts that must rend the breast of him who gave me being, receive my thanks.—My name is De Courci; in the west of England stands the mansion of my ancestors."

"What is thine?" said the Lord Montmoreci, turning to Leonard, whose cheek blushed a deep crimson at the question.

"My name and birth," replied the youth, "are humble; upon the estate of Lord Fitzallan, in fair Northumberland, I drew my earliest breath."

"My friend," cried the Baron, addressing himself to the follower of Leonard, "I do not know your name."

"Truly, my Lord," replied Owen, "my name is not very well known as yet, not having had an opportunity of distinguishing myself by any bold atchievements; nor are my parents in affluence. *Like master, like man,* you will say. Though I could shew your Lordship a file of ancestors as long as a chain of Welch mountains! First, there was the great Ap Hugh; from him descended the renowned Ap Price, who gave birth to Ap Griffin; after them comes Ap Williams; then Ap Hume; all of which center in the present Owen Ap Lewyn, distantly related to the great Prince Lewellyn."

"I thank you for the recital of your pedigree," interrupted the Baron, with a smile, "though I must own, I before thought there was something noble in your manner."

"Yes, I have often been told so," quoth the 'Squire, conceitedly.

"Well then, you will oblige me," returned Montmorenci, "by desiring the Steward to attend me in the oaken parlour, that I may give him instructions to prepare messengers to convey my guests letters."

So saying, he departed from the room, while Edgar wrote to his father, and Leonard indicted a billet to old Christopher, and another to Emma.

CHAPTER XI

O sacred fire that burnest mightily
    In living beasts, ykindled first above,
Amongst th'eternal spheres and lamping sky,
And thence pour'd in men, which men call love;
Not that same which doth base affections move
    In brutish mindes, and filthy lust inflame;
But that sweet fit, that does true beauty love,
    And choseth virtue for his dearest dame,
    Whence spring all noble deeds, and never-dying fame.
                                        SPENSER.

LONG they had not sojourned at the Isle of Wight, 'ere Leonard discovered in De Courci, a thoughtfulness he could not account for; and about which he resolved to interrogate him, the first opportunity that offered. This he soon had; strolling from the castle, he descried Edgar, stretched on the grass, beneath the shadow of a lofty pine; he seemed lost in reverie; nor did he perceive his friend, until he inquired the cause of his being in so retired a spot.

De Courci, with an embarrassed air, replied, "The heat of the weather had driven him to seek the shelter of that friendly tree."

"In vain," quoth Leonard, "you attempt to deceive me; some secret anguish preys upon your spirits, to which I am a stranger: impart your grief, the lenient hand of friendship may administer some consolation; and, should that pleasure be denied me, be assured your recital shall be locked in the cabinet of my bosom, of which you yourself shall keep the key."

"Thou art, indeed, a friend!" cried Edgar, "and yet I am ashamed to own my weakness. Know, then, I love the gentle Julia from my soul; yea, idolize her. On our first interview, in distant Gallia, I sucked the fatal poison, but strove to conquer my rash passion; which, since her unexpected presence here,

69

has gained so great an ascendency, I vainly strive to shake it off, for it will end but in the grave."

"And call you this a weakness?" exclaimed Leonard, with energy; "if so, you are indeed unworthy of the lady's love. No! make it your boast; for sure, if boasting may be licenced, it is when an enraptured lover proclaims the beauties of his mistress."

"Alas!" returned De Courci, "you know not what I have endured! since first I saw the heavenly enchantress, sleep has been as great a stranger to these eyes, as comfort to the wretch condemned to waste his life in hopeless bondage. I should, 'ere this, have made my passion known, and claimed, at least, some share of her soft pity, but that I fear the pensive turn, with which nature has marked my disposition, must appear unseemly in the eyes of one possessed of such vivacity. Judge then——"

"And is it possible," interrupted Leonard, "that, uncertain of the sentiments of her you love, you thus become a victim of despair? Shake off this mental lethargy; disclose to her the flame with which your bosom burns, and sue for a return: should she prove averse to your fond wishes, it will then be time enough to yield yourself a prey to misery."

Edgar, somewhat comforted by this remonstrance, promised to profit by his friend's advice, and returned with him to the castle.

In the evening, the Baron Montmorenci and his lady, having quitted the hall, the son of Christopher found means to retire, leaving De Courci with Julia. They were no sooner alone, than, in a tremulous voice, he thus addressed her.

"Forgive, charming creature, the abruptness of what I am about to say, nor let me lose the small share of your esteem, that I flatter myself I at present possess, by a rash declaration. Have I your permission to speak?—Say yes, and make me blest."

70

"Indeed," said she, "I have no commission from his holiness; nor did I ever know it was in my power to bestow a blessing: but if it is comprised in so small a compass as a monosyllable, take it.—Yes!"

"Adorable lady!" cried Edgar, "deign to listen to me. From the first moment I beheld you, my heart has been your slave: tasteless and insipid is every pleasure to me; and, unless you condescend to bid me hope, my happiness is forever blasted. To my native country I bid an eternal adieu, and spend the sad remainder of my days in voluntary banishment. But wheresoever I turn my wandering steps, whether amidst the scorching climes of distant India, or the drizzling snow of Lapland, still your lov'd image shall accompany me, and cheer my solitary hours."

"I am not," replied the fair one, "quite so cruel as to wish to sacrifice your peace to my own vanity; nor do I wish my name to be handed down to posterity, by the appellation of the hardhearted maiden, who forced a noble youth to quit his country for love! to be plain, I am far from disliking you; procure the sanction of those who have a prior right to me, and, I do not think I shall drive you to desperation."

Edgar dropped on his knee, and pressed her hand with fervency to his lips; then hurried in quest of Leonard, whom he made acquainted with his success; and, at the same time, besought him to use his interest with Montmorenci, to procure his assent.

They both instantly repaired to their noble host, and opened their suit. He listened with attention to them, and frankly owned, there was no man he would so soon call son, as De Courci; but, at the same time, forbade his speaking more on the subject, till he had obtained his father's approbation; to whom Edgar wrote, and had the satisfaction to receive the accord of his parent.

All was now happiness at the castle; pleasure, with her mirthful train, seemed to have made it her abode: joy wantoned in every countenance, save young Leonard's, whose features forced a momentary smile; like to the moon, when through a watery cloud she makes her way to cheer the benighted traveller, and is again obscured by vapours. He was a captive in the chains of love: the thought of his beloved Emma, like the Promethean vulture, preyed upon his vitals, and banished peace from his disordered mind.

Each succeeding day was spent at the castle in nearly the same manner as the preceding one; their first, their last, and constant care, was to return thanks to the Almighty disposer of all events, for his wonderous bounty. The morning was employed by the Baron, and his young visitants, in hunting, and other manly exercises: by Julia, and her mother, in wandering through the cottages of the tenants, and relieving the wants of age and infancy. Nor was their charity unrewarded; the sympathizing tear that stole imperceptibly down their cheek, on relieving a distressed innocent from unmerited misery, was a source of greater bliss to them, than all the noisy mirth and splendour of a court. The latter part of the day was entirely devoted to the ladies; they rode, walked, or diverted themselves with angling in a lake that laid at the back of the castle.

One evening, while they were employed in the latter amusement, Julia stumbled over the root of an old oak, that spread itself along the bank, and fell into the water. Edgar, unmindful of his own safety, and anxious only for that of his mistress, plunged in to save her.

Her father, who with Leonard, was at some distance, perceiving the perilous situation of his child, ran to afford her aid, and arrived at the spot from which she had fallen, at the instant that De Courci brought her in his arms to shore. They conveyed her, almost lifeless, to the castle, and she was immediately put to bed by her afflicted mother; while Edgar was in a state of mind not to be described; and the Baron, notwithstanding his own grief, was obliged to use every means in his power to mitigate that of his friend.

In the course of a few hours, Julia gave signs of returning life; which welcome news was instantly made known to the Knights, accompanied by a message from their noble hostess, requesting to see them both the next morning, when she hoped her daughter would be able to express her gratitude to her generous deliverer. On receiving this consoling intelligence, they bade adieu, and parted.

Owen attended his master to his chamber, and instantly entered into conversation.

"I hope, sir," cried the Squire, "you will not be offended at what I am about to say, but I can be silent no longer; and a man may as well be killed as frightened to death. In short, I am firmly bent on making my escape from this place, the very first opportunity that offers. Zounds, if such things happen often, *By the valour of my ancestors!* I would not stay to be made Lord of the island."

"What ails thee?" replied his master, "the accident you allude to might indeed have been fatal; thank heaven it proved otherwise! but, had the lady perished, I know your gallantry would not have prompted you to aid her."

"You cannot tell that," quoth Owen, "But how comes it, sir, your gallantry did not whisper you to assist her?"

"I was at a distance," returned Leonard, "and ran immediately to her relief."

"Yes," cried his follower, "but you know you might have made a little more haste if you would."

The Knight smiled at the retort, and answered, "I did not know your feelings were so fine. And is this your reason for wishing to depart?"

"Oh! no!" exclaimed Owen, "I am very sorry for the poor lady to be sure; but my fears arise from a different cause. I am certain the castle is haunted; for coming through the gallery to night in the dark, I espied a light through a key-hole: Ho! ho!" says I to myself, "this leads to some apartment; but, instead of that, it opened into the chapel, where the first thing that I saw, was an undescribable kind of being, at the altar, more like a devil than a man, dressed in black, with large eyes, fire at his nostrils, and a huge pair of whiskers, as large as a Turk's. I need not tell you my courage forsook me a little: By the valor of my ancestors! nay, and St. David, and the whole catalogue of champions to boot, I shook like an aspen leaf, and tottered out much faster than I entered. Now you may make light of it, if you please; but I myself am not fond of strange company, and always had a violent antipathy to capering goblins."

"Blockhead!" interrupted his master, "your fears have conjured up this phœnomenon."

"And pray, sir, was it my fears that conjured up the phœ— mo—: what is it? I mean the ghost at Fitzallan's mansion."

"No trifling," quoth the Knight, "but come, attend me to the chapel, and let me have ocular demonstration that there is truth in your assertion. Follow me!"

"No," replied Owen, "if I do, brand me for a coward! I'll not run my head into danger: and let me tell you, sir, if you was to get old father Anselm to lay it in the red sea, (for that is the burial place, they tell me, for all spirit's bodies) it would be much better than paying your respects to it: take my word you will be brought in as an accomplice; and then they will burn you for a Wizard, as poor Hugh, the Currier of Glamorgan, was served.—I will tell you a story about that affair; I had it from my father. You must know there was an old Witch that used——"

"Peace! foolish paltroon!" cried Leonard, "then tarry here till I return."

"In good sooth," said the Squire, "if that is the case, I am afraid I shall wait long enough."

"Silence, ideot!" exclaimed his master, taking a taper, and drawing his falchion, "and direct me to the chapel."

Owen went into the gallery, and, having pointed out the door he had discovered, locked himself in the chamber of Leonard, who entered the sacred place; where, immediately, the solemn, mellow strains of the organ vibrated on his ear, and rolled through the several aisles, till, lost in distance, they were heard no more. Astonishment took possession of his faculties! Was it possible any person could, at so unseasonable an hour, visit the cold damp pavement of a place like that? And if so, for what purpose? These ideas perplexed him; nevertheless, he approached, and beheld a figure descend the stairs of the choir, and suddenly vanish through a door, which it immediately closed, and was opposite to that Leonard entered at.

He endeavoured to open it, but to no purpose; then, much chagrined, repaired to his own apartment, and was congratulated by Owen on his escape, as he termed it.

"Well, sir," said he, "was it my fears conjured up this Demon?"

"I confess," answered the Knight, "there is something more than fancy in what you told me."

"I *fancy* so indeed," cried his follower, "and I *fancy* that it is the *fancy* of this dev,—I mean this gentleman with the cloven foot, to frighten us all to death!"

"No more," interrupted Leonard, "but this: let me entreat you to conceal your idle fears from the domesticks, nor drop a syllable of what has passed. To-morrow night I am fixed on discovering the mystery that attends the chapel."

He then dismissed his 'Squire, and retired to his couch.

CHAPTER XII

Let us with silent footsteps go
To charnels, and the house of woe;
To gothic churches, vaults, and tombs,
Where each sad night some virgin comes,
With throbbing heart, and faded cheek,
Her promis'd bridegroom's urn to seek.
WHARTON.

IN the mean while the afflicted Edgar, with anxiety, waited the return of day; and scarce did the golden axles of the ruddy god dart above the eastern hills, 'ere he arose, and repaired to the chamber of Leonard.

"Pardon this early intrusion," he said, "but the solicitude I have undergone since yester-evening, has deprived me of rest: my couch is comfortless, and the only satisfaction I can experience, must be in your society."

The son of Christopher instantly arose, and accompanied his friend to the sea-beach, where they walked till the usual hour of the families rising; they then returned, and sent to inquire if they might be permitted to pay their respects to the ladies: the answer was, the Baroness and Julia would be happy to see them in the apartment of the latter, who was so much recovered as to be able to leave her bed.

On entering the room, De Courci could no longer conceal his feelings, but threw himself upon his knees before his mistress, and, pressing her hand to his lips, exclaimed, "Charming Julia! did you know the torture I have suffered, since I last beheld you, you might form an idea of the passion that consumes me."

She replied, "It is impossible for words to convey the thanks that are your due; and, in sooth, I am a very indifferent orator at best: all, then, I can offer you, is my heart, of which you

76

have, indeed, long been master; and the warmth of whose affection, the frigid water has not had power to abate."

"She is yours," said her father, "had I a thousand daughters, and a thousand kingdoms to bestow on them, I would wish none a happier lot."

De Courci considered himself over-paid, by the thanks he received from this truly noble family; and experienced peculiar satisfaction in having contributed to their happiness.

During the day, Owen contrived to mount his favourite hobby, and was, as usual, indebted to the fertility of his own brain for the narrations he related. He recounted battles that had never taken place, and slew heroes that never had existence.

"This is all mighty fine talk," quoth Jeremy the Steward, "but do not you think it much better to live at home in quiet, than to cut one another in pieces? If you look out from the south gallery window, you will see the flocks grazing: pretty things! Oh, I often wish to be a lamb!"

"A what," cried Owen, "a lamb? No, nature very plainly designed you for an ass; nor in this instance has her plan been thwarted. *By the valour of my ancestors!* you have no more heart than a tom-tit; though to be sure every man is not blest with courage. But, what the deuce, would you have a person waste his life in solitude, and then, as you are, be kept like part of the armour in the great hall, merely for the sake of antiquity? I know nothing to be sure: but this I do know, that I would recommend the profession of arms to all young men."

Thus did the 'Squire boast, although, at the same time, he would rather have had the command of a good pantry, and a well stored cellar of wine, than have been constituted generalissimo of half the forces in Europe.

Mean-while, the tedious hours appeared of double length to the impetuous Leonard, who ardently tarried the tolling of the curfew, as he determined again to repair unto the chapel, and endeavour to develope the mystery that waited on it. At length the wished for night appeared, and, at the usual time of retirement, Owen attended his master, as had been ordered, and sought, by every argument, to put him from his purpose.

"So, sir," he exclaimed, "you are going to make one in the chapel. But do, for the blessed Virgin's sake, before it is too late, consider what you are about; and, if this strange gentleman must amuse himself in nightly revels, pray, if you have any interest, persuade him to hold them somewhere else; for instance, at the neighbouring convent: I am told the Monks are fine jolly fellows, and you know there he will not disturb any one, there are so many of his own kidney."

"Blockhead," said Leonard, "will you never divest yourself of these unmanly, cowardly ideas? What is there I should fear? I have done no one an injury, and, I trust, the Omnipotent Being, who has so often led me through the carnage of battle, will never forsake me while I deserve his protection."

"True," replied his follower, "but you know it is wrong to be too troublesome; and I am certain, were I to run myself into as many dangers as you do, I should be so often upon my knees, that my prayers would be wholly disregarded."

The hoarse and brazen voice of the castle clock, now chiming, stopped this harangue, and warned Leonard of his intention.

It was at the dark and dismal hour of night, when churchyards yawn, and vomit forth the restless spirits of the dead, to shake the conscience of the murderer; when the "shard-born beetle" wheels his droney hum, and bats through cloistered churches flit their way, disturbing the silent mansion of those deceased; when the nightly, and portentous screech owl flaps against the casement of the sickly wretch, and warns him to prepare for his sad end: at the lonely time when witches solemnize pale Hecate's festival, by the reflex of Cynthia's beams,

Leonard once more entered the chapel, and beheld the same figure.

Being somewhat more collected, he exclaimed, "Who art thou?" when the object before him uttered a loud shriek, and sunk upon the pavement. He instantly ran to the spot, and, touching the supposed phantom, had the felicity to find it was no shadow, but his dear, his living Emma!

Their joy, on meeting, cannot be described, and, for a time, prevented Leonard the power of articulation: at length he entreated his beloved to disclose the happy means that so unexpectedly blest him with her sight.

"Alas!" quoth the maid, "persecution has driven me from my home, and forced me to become a wandering exile."

"Persecution, said'st thou?" exclaimed her lover, "tell me but the name of those who have dared to injure innocence like thine; and, fear not, but they shall dearly atone their savage cruelty."

"Be calm," returned Emma, "and you shall know all. A short time back, I was surprised by the arrival of a stranger at our cottage, richly caparisoned, and attended by a numerous retinue; he desired a private conference with my father, which was granted, and was of long continuance. At the conclusion the guest departed, and my parent, in a serious tone, addressed me in the following words."

"You know, Emma, what pains I have taken to rear you; and you also know, in your happiness consists my own. You have now the power, and I hope you will not neglect it, of making me some return for all the cares I lavished on you, and to lay up my hours to come in peace and plenty."

"An involuntary horror seized me as he spoke, though unconscious of the cause, and made me tremble like the palsied leaves, when ruffled by the passing gale!"

"Thou dost not answer me," continued my father.

"I faintly replied, You have put no question to me: it is true, you have declared I can make you a recompense for your past tenderness: tell me then how, and I shall be happy?"

"Thou art a good girl," quoth he, "mark me, this stranger is a Knight of wide domain, and Lord of many vassals: he has solicited your hand, which in your name I have promised him."

"I could hear no more, my senses were benumbed, and I fell into a swoon. When I revived, I found my father busy in attending me, although his features were much distorted by rage and disappointment.

"He instantly renewed the subject," saying, "No more of this childish play: you must, you shall be his."

"Never!" interrupted I, "Though I were dragged unto the altar, where many a victim has preceded me; nay, though the irrevocable ceremony were performed, and the fatal ring placed on my trembling hand, my heart would still befriend me, and death should put a period to my sufferings!"

"By the blessed Mary!" exclaimed my parent, "this is too much! my authority despised even to my face! But prepare for the alternative: you marry this Knight, who degrades himself by seeking the alliance, or quit my cottage and protection for ever!"

"He then left me to my sorrows.

"When I could summon fortitude to reflect, I cast my eyes upon the dreary prospect around me, and could see nought but a wilderness of misery: almost distracted, I knew not how to act; when thy dear loved remembrance, like a friendly beacon to the sea-tossed mariner, came to my tortured fancy, and rescued me from the tremendous precipice whereon I tottered. I instantly resolved to fly my home, and, knowing from your letter, you were on this island, to throw myself under your protection. My plan was no sooner formed than executed; I quitted the vale that night, doubly regreting the loss of my deceased mother, and in a state little short of frenzy.

"The paly glow-worm lighted my lonely way, till dawn appeared upon the misty mountain's top, chasing away the chilling dews of night, and invigorating nature. I pursued my course, and at length embarked for the Isle of Wight.

"On landing, I was accosted by an aged fisherman, who requested I would accept some refreshment at his cottage. I joyfully embraced the invitation, and accompanied him home, where I was as well entertained as his fare would permit.

"My kind host then inquired to what part I was destined. A blush suffused my cheek at this question, which I scarce could answer; at length I informed him, it was my desire to get admitted as a domestic in the mansion of the Lord Montmorenci. He replied, I could not have applied to any one who had more interest there than himself; and, so saying, went from the cottage; but returning in a short time, told me the superintendant of the castle would be happy to see me, and I immediately set out for this place, where I have since remained, hoping, by your manner, to discover whether all traces of your Emma were worn from your remembrance.

"As my chamber adjoins this holy place, I embraced the opportunity of offering up my oraisons to that fount, from whence, alone, comfort can flow. Last night I was alarmed by the sight of a man, as I left the choir: fear impressed me, and caused me to fly swift as my frame would suffer me. The dawn, however, dispelled my apprehensions, and my confident trust in heaven made me determine again to visit the chapel; I did so, and imagine you, who have ever been the object of my love, was then unwittingly the source of my terror!"

Leonard having affirmed he was the person who had innocently alarmed her, related the various incidents that had befallen him since their parting; in which he had hardly made a conclusion, when the door that opened from the gallery, creek'd on its hinges, and presently the voice of Owen echoed through the chapel, who cried, in a loud whisper, "Sir! sir! are you safe?"

"Enter," returned his master, "here are none but friends."

He peeped in, but discovering Emma, was about to retire.

"What," said Leonard, "Are you frightened at a woman?"

"At what!" exclaimed the 'Squire, returning, "A woman! a woman? I frightened! not at the devil. Oh! oh! now I can account for your determination to fathom the mystery of the chapel. In good truth, had I thought it had been haunted by such a beautiful spirit, I should have made no objection to accompanying you."

"Hold," interrupted the Knight, "why sure you dream! this is the undescribable being with large eyes!——"

"Ah! my dear sir, for heaven's sake stop!" cried Owen, "*By the valour of my Ancestors!* this is like reprieving a man at the gibbet, and hanging him on the next tree. I hope, madam, you will pardon the description I gave of you, but it really was occasioned by fear—that is—not absolutely fear—though I believe it was something devilish like it—a kind of panic, to which the boldest of us warriors are liable at times."

"Spare your observations," quoth his master, "and now, my lovely Emma, farewell till the morrow, when I will introduce you to my noble host, and his worthy family, who will, I am right sure, feel pleasure in being enabled to offer an asylum to innocence, labouring under the persecution of parental tyranny."

Then taking leave, they retired; not to rest, but to enjoy the reflection of the past scene. Leonard, on the ensuing morn, entered the hall with a chearful countenance; his noble friends observed his joy, and, being made acquainted with the last night's adventure, requested to be introduced to his mistress.

On her entering the room, they could not marvel that his heart had been enslaved by one possessed of so much beauty: never, indeed, was there a greater assemblage of charms; her lovely form was cast in nature's choicest mould; her intelligent eyes beamed mildness and benignity, while the long auburn locks that shaded a neck, white as the swan, and transparent as the crystal stream whereon he sails, were beautiful beyond description. Notwithstanding, her personal accomplishments fell short of the graces that adorned her mind, which, it is sufficient to say, was the abode of innocence and virtue.

The addition of such an inmate at the castle, could not but be acceptable to its noble inhabitants. Leonard, and his adored mistress, experienced the satisfaction so justly their due; their happiness seemed solid; but such is the sublunary state of human life, that, when they thought themselves compleatly blessed, a long and painful separation, like the still calm before an approaching storm, was preparing for them.

About this time Edgar received a letter from his father, requiring his presence, and accompanied by a fervent invitation to his friend. The former presented the billet to Montmorenci, and added, "that he was compelled to take his leave on the ensuing day."

The Baron entreated him to prolong his stay, but De Courci, although his heart was rivetted to the spot which contained his mistress, yet, now that the commands of a parent summoned him, resigned himself to duty and filial affection.

The mind of Leonard, on this occasion, was torn by contending passions: the necessity of his return to England was obvious; as the authors of his being certainly had a claim upon him; but the idea of where he should dispose his Emma, during his absence, much tormented him. The amiable Julia, however, quickly dispelled his anxiety, and banished melancholy from his breast.

"My charming friend," said she to Emma, "we cannot so soon consent to part with your society: you must remain with us, and, while these Knights-errants are ploughing the boisterous deep, and rescuing damsels from distress, we will pray together for their safety."

Leonard gladly caught at the invitation, and was happy to leave his mistress to the care of such distinguished characters. A load was taken off his mind, and again pleasure sparkled in his eye. He thought fit, however, to leave his 'Squire as an attendant upon Emma; and when he informed him of his design, and added a strict injunction that he should pay her every attention, Owen replied,

"Fear not but I will serve her with the same assiduity as yourself; and will protect her as nobly as my great grand-father Lewellyn could do, were he alive. *By the valour of my Ancestors!* should any one offend her, they shall taste the flavour of my rapier; and, I have a notion, they will find it rather hard of digestion: this is the very weapon that great prince wore at——"

Leonard smiled at this harangue, and having entreated his 'Squire to act up to what he professed, left him.

CHAPTER XIII

——Oh, the curse of marriage!
That we can call these delicate creatures ours,
And not their appetites. I had rather be a toad,
And live upon the vapour of a dungeon,
Than keep a corner in the thing I love,
For other's use.

SHAKESPEARE.

Neither man nor angel can discern
Hypocrisy, the only evil that walks
Invisible, except to God alone.——

MILTON.

THE Knights took a tender leave of the Baron, and his family, and, on the following day, quitted the castle. When Leonard bade his mistress farewell, she could scarce return an answer, so much was her susceptible heart affected. She presented him, at parting, with a white scarf, worked by her own fingers, as a memorial of her love; and he vowed never to resign it, but with his latest breath!

They then proceeded to the sea shore, near which the vessel lay wherein they were to embark; and on the beach they met Peter, who accosted them.

"Well, your honours," he cried, "what you are homeward bound, hey? The wind and weather is fairer than it was when you landed here: shiver my bowsprit! but it blew great guns that night! however, I fancy you have had a tight birth on't at the Barons: good messing I take it!"

"We have met with unparalleled hospitality," replied Edgar, "but our gratitude is not confined to him alone; for had not you kindly informed him of our misfortune, he had still been ignorant of it."

"Avast, your honour!" said the fisherman, "clap your compliments under hatches; why I know no more of the lingo you
are talking, than the sheet-anchor-stock; or, damme! than a
French Mounseer knows the taste of roast beef!"

"You are a noble fellow!" quoth Leonard, "and I once more
entreat you to accept some recompense for your disinterested
generosity."

"No," returned Peter, "I cannot: I am a volunteer in these
cases, and would scorn to accept bounty-money for merely
performing a common act of charity. Heaven bless you, my
masters! may the winds of adversity never shatter your hulks,
but may you sail, with a fair breeze, down the current of life,
and cast the anchor of your latter days in the port of prosperity!"

With these words he departed, while the Knights embarked; and were no sooner on board, than the white sails were
set to catch the breath of zephyr, which soon wafted them to
the rugged clifts of Albion's sea-girt shore. They then mounted
their horses, and, in a short time, gained the dwelling of De
Courci, who welcomed them with equal warmth and affection.

The hours passed upon the downy wings of pleasure, and
nought imbittered those of Leonard, and his friend, but the soft
image of their absent loves. They anticipated, however, the
pleasure of again meeting them, and cheered the spirits of each
other, by ever dwelling on their favourite theme.

Thus were they situated, when one day that Leonard was
employed in fruitless attempts to decypher the characters on
the back of the miniature, given him by Christopher, he descried an horseman, riding at full speed towards the castle; and
from his appearance, judged it to be his 'Squire; but reason
forbade his encouraging the idea: he had left him in the Isle of
Wight, it was therefore impossible. His conjecture, however,
was confirmed, for, on a near approach, he plainly discovered
the features of Owen.

He instantly rushed into the court-yard, and exclaimed to his servant, who dismounted, "In the name of the blessed Trinity! what hast thou to impart?"

"In truth," returned the 'Squire, "I have not breath to impart any thing, I have lost it all by the way."

"This is no time for trifling!" cried the Knight, in an angry tone; "follow me, and ease the torturing suspense that racks my heart, or woe upon thee!"

Owen bowed, and attended Leonard to his closet, who said, "Now speak, void of thy ill-timed gibes, or dread my just resentment!"

"Why," quoth the attendant, "I would have told you all, if you had given me time, and, like a skilful doctor, would have administered medicine, to enable you to undergo the operation with patience."

"Wretch!" interrupted the son of Christopher, "Is this thy boasted regard? But proceed; tell me the cause of thy being here, or by him who gave me life, this instant is your last!"

"I am afraid it will, without your kind assistance," replied the servant, "but prepare for the worst, if you will have it so: your mistress is stolen from the castle of Montmorenci; by whom no one can tell; all we know is, she was put on board a boat by several men, who carried her off in less time than would truss a rabbit."

Had a dagger been planted in the breast of Leonard, it could not more have pained him.

"And is it possible," he cried, "you cannot guess what is become of her?"

Owen shook his head, and sighed.

With folded arms, and his brow contracted with grief and indignation, the Knight threw himself into a chair, and continued buried in painful reverie; then, starting suddenly from his seat, he fell upon his knees and ejaculated.

"Almighty Father! listen and record my fixed resolve; never shall this frame know happiness, till the accursed authors of this horrid sacrilege are punished! Kneeling, I vow to dedicate my life to her revenge! And thou, oh fortune! blind and fickle Deity! also hear my prayer: befriend me in this trying hour; reveal to me the name of her detested persecutor; bring us but point to point, and as thou pleasest, then bestow thy smiles!"

While he spoke, his countenance was flushed with rage; his eye-balls rolled in their sockets, and his mind resembled the tempestuous ocean when Boreas' blasts convulse the watery gulph.

"Caparison my charger!" cried he, "even now will I commence my search: every moment that I lose is a treason to love!"

Owen replied, "Truly sir, if I may presume to advise, it will be better to postpone your journey till the morning; consider, it is not now far from dark, and while that is the case, you may as well attempt to catch a will o' th' wisp! Besides, to say sooth, my courage is very apt to leave me by night; it is like an intermitting fever, comes and goes so quick, that I cannot be certain of it for a moment together. Do, for heaven's sake, let us wait till dawn."

This persuasion had the desired effect; the impetuous Leonard consented to tarry [till] daylight; on which the 'Squire withdrew, in order to recruit his exhausted strength; while his master remained a prey to anguish.

A few hours after, the Baron, in passing through the gallery of the castle, heard the buz of conversation in his lady's apartment, the door of which was open: advancing, he beheld her on her knees, entreating some man, whose features he could not distinguish, to spare her honour, though her life were the alternative. De Courci instantly rushed into the room; but oh! what pen can do justice to his feelings, when he saw Gertrude struggling to disengage herself from the hold of Leonard. Not all the influence of the Gorgon's head could more effectually have deprived him of motion: he stood fixed to the spot, and tongue-tied by surprise; while his consort rushed into his arms, exclaiming, "Oh! save me! save me!"

For a time the whole group remained in silence; at length the Baron, fixing his eyes on Leonard, thus addressed him.

"Were I not myself a witness of your atrocious villany, not all the powers of the universe could cause me to believe it were possible. Is this the return for all the kindness I have lavished on you? I have been nursing a serpent in my bosom, which now repays me with the sharp venom of its cankered tooth. What punishment, just heaven, is equal to his crime? Without there—"

Several domesticks appeared, to whom he thus continued.

"Attend, and mark my orders: drag yon ungrateful wretch to the tower near the postern-gate; load him with irons, and, on your lives, see that all light be secluded from his cell; in darkness let him brood over his guilt, and learn the recompense of black ingratitude."

Gertrude threw herself upon her knees, her eyes brimful of sorrow, and cried, "Alas! my Lord! hear my petition; and, as your indulgent nature has never yet refused the boon I asked, Oh! see me thus enforce it at your feet: confine him not; far from the dwelling of his injured benefactor let him shape his way, and leave to Providence the reward of his offence.

"Arise," said the Baron, softened by this address, "on thy account I mitigate my rigour. Convey him according to my orders, but manacle him not; for sure, if conscience can gain admittance to his callous heart, all corporeal weight will be superfluous! Ask me no further, nor put me to the pain of denying you. Bear him away, it shocks my sight to think that nature should have stamped the form of man on such a monster."

The servants approached to seize the Knight, who, drawing his sword with unparalleled valour, held them long at bay; but, overpowered by numbers, his courage was fruitless; they captured him, and, spite of his struggle, dragged him to prison.

Several days now rolled on at the castle, without any occurrence worthy of being mentioned, when a misfortune happened, which threw the whole mansion into a state of confusion.

The worthy owner had retired to his couch, but sleep was banished from his lids; nor when the chiming clock beat two, had he scarce closed his eyes: the taper twinkled in the socket, and at last expired, when he heard footsteps creeping into his apartment: while he lay perplexed in conjecture, the curtains were undrawn, and, in the same moment, he received a wound, which fortunately only grazed his arm. Suddenly he wrenched the dagger, and plunged it into the body of the midnight assassin; then called aloud for lights: the servants flew with them; but better had their Lord for ever remained in darkness; for, in the features of the murderer, he discovered his own wife!

What a sight for an husband, who professed the tenderest affection for his consort, and from whom alone he hoped for happiness, or misery! he gazed with a sensation not to be described; while the Baroness, turning her eyes towards him, faintly cried, "Can I, oh! can I ask forgiveness of one I have so basely injured? Yet, so well I know your noble disposition, that, as a few short moments only stand 'twixt me and dread eternity, you will not let me vainly plead for pardon, nor embitter the few remaining moments, even of a wretch like me, by withholding the consolation which it is in your power to give."

De Courci, with the assistance of his domestics, placed her on a couch, and ordered them to procure immediate assistance.

"Not for your lives," exclaimed Gertrude, "death is the only friend I can now rely on, and, as I feel his hasty stride, listen all, and profit by my confession. Infidelity to your bed, my Lord, was my first, and shocking as it may appear, my least offence. You cannot have forgotten; Alas! too well do I remember it! When you left your own mansion for that of Fitzallan; during your absence that villain visited me, and, with all the subtilty of marked hypocrisy, entreated permission to remain my safeguard. Unconscious of his purpose, I consented. What can I say? In one unguarded, fatal moment, I sacrificed my honour, and your own, to that arch fiend.

"When virtue once has taken a step down the deep, tremendous crag of vice, it is easier far to descend the dangerous precipice, than by a firm and steady resolution, seek to prevent the ill effects of what is passed: step by step we are, imperceptibly, led on in error, and, hardly ever pause, till we reach the gloomy valley of perdition!

"Such was my case: had I stopped there, all might have been as well, as a mind torn by compunction, could be: nor would your heart have ever felt the pangs I see this knowledge of my offence occasions. Still, surely, when you know the summit of my baseness, you will bless Providence, that, by your hand, cuts off a wretch unfit to live.

"In an illicit intercourse with Edmund did I continue, till your letters informed me you were returning victorious from the borders. The praises which you lavished on your youthful soldier, caused me, with double impatience, to await your return: the hour at last arrived, that sealed my destiny; the instant I beheld the gallant Leonard, love's fiery torch consumed my heart, and has ever since burned with increasing fury in my breast.

"During his first sojourn here, I panted to declare my passion; but the service of his country called him from us, and with an aching heart, I saw him quit these walls. Absence, the accustomed antidote of lovers, increased the heat within my bosom, and I languished for his return. He came, an hero, crowned with laurel, the pride of England, and his friends.

"I could no longer conceal my adulterous passion; and, on the evening of his 'Squire's arrival, passing his chamber, I beheld him bathed in tears: yes, his manly eyes were suffused with drops of sorrow; and sobs of anguish burst from his tortured breast. I could not bear to view him thus; like gentle breezes on the glowing embers, it added fire to the flame, and I requested an interview in my own apartment; first exacting from him a solemn vow, never to impart the subject of our converse. He attended, and in one moment I forgot the dignity of my sex; the duty that I owed my Lord, and every earthly, every heavenly tie.—I confessed I loved him.

"The astonished youth could hardly speak: at length;"—"I know not," he replied, "what answer it befits me to make; or whether to retire, and leave you to your own reflection. But, as you hope for everlasting peace, stifle this horrid infatuation, which is an ill requital for the Baron's profuse tenderness! the secret, I hope I need not tell you, remains with me as though I had never known it: I would I never had!"

"Seeing he was about to depart," continued Gertrude, "I fell upon my knees, and conjured him not to leave me: at that instant I descried you at the door, and converted my suppliant situation to my own advantage; happy to be avenged on Leonard, whose indifference stung me to the heart. You know what followed; by my arts did that deserving young man become the inmate of a noisome dungeon: compunction, I must own, then seized me, but my love, deaf as the wind to every cry of conscience, hurried me on; and considering you, my Lord, the only obstacle that stood 'twixt me and my desires, I formed the dreadful resolution of destroying you; and this night entered your chamber, to put my accursed plan in execution; but, I thank the disposer of all things, I fell in my own snare!"

The wretched Gertrude again solicited forgiveness of De Courci.

"If my pardon," exclaimed the benignant husband, "can aught avail, or smooth your passage to the other world, look up secure of it; and may you experience the same mercy from an offended Deity!"

"Heaven eternally bless you!" cried she, "one thing more; Leonard was by me———"

Here her voice failed: she clasped her hands, while, like a dying taper that now glimmers, now is lost, her soul trembled in its mortal socket: at length the spark of life expired, and she breathed her last, "*With all her imperfections on her head!*"

The Baron bedewed the body of his unhappy consort with many a tear; and then, attended by his domestics, hastened to liberate the captive Leonard. They opened his prison door, and called upon his name, but no answer was received, save the responsive notes of echo! they then entered, and searched, but all in vain; the dungeon was evacuated, yet were there no traces of his escape.

Gertrude's last words now struck Edgar, and he imparted the same to his father, who suspected that ill-fated youth had fallen by her revengeful arm. He quitted the cell, having given orders that diligent quest should be made after the Knight; offering, also, a reward to any that should bring tidings of him; though, at the same time, De Courci feared, if he ever again beheld him, it would be no longer the blooming, gallant Leonard, but a pale inanimate corpse.

END OF VOLUME ONE.

THE
M Y S T E R Y
OF THE
Black Tower

CHAPTER I

Nought is there under heaven's wide hollowness
That moves more dear compassion of mind,
Than beauty brought to unworthy wretchedness
By envy's snares, or fortune's freaks unkind.
I, whether lately thro' her brightness blind,
Or thro' allegiance and fast fealty,
Which I do owe unto all woman-kind,
Feel my heart pierc'd with so great agony,
When such I see, that all for pity I could die.

SPENSER.

Virtue would see to do what virtue would
By her own radiant light, though sun and moon
Were in the flat sea-sunk.

MILTON.

WE now recur to Emma, who so suddenly disappeared from the Isle of Wight. She had been walking on the beach with Julia, and contemplating nature's bounteous picture. The island presented to their sight a luxurious landscape, adorned with enamelled meadows, whereon the herd, in wanton gambol, nipped their verdant food; the ocean, scarcely ruffled by a breath of zephyr, was smooth and glassy; while, in the western horizon, the golden rays of the departing phœbus danced on its watery bosom, and the white cliffs of Albion finished this enchanting scene; in which they were so lost, that they thought not of returning till the falling mist, and the decrease of light, cautioned them to retrace their steps; they did so, but, as they proceeded, their way was obstructed by a band of armed men, who seized on Emma, and forced her, spite of her tears and shrieks, into a shallop, leaving Julia upon the sands, wringing her hands in anguish, and conjuring them, by every solemn adjuration, to release her friend. Deaf alike to the solicitations of both, the ruffians spread their sail, and bore away their prize; who, with all the eloquence of beauty, entreated them to tell her where she was going, and for what purpose?

"You will know that hereafter," replied one of them; which was the only answer she could gain; her sighs passed unregarded on the floating breeze, and as well might she have craved pity from the furious tiger, as have moved the stony hearts of those unfeeling wretches.

On the second night they made their destined port, and went on shore, having previously placed a bandage over the eyes of their victim. They continued their walk for some time, and ascended several flights of stairs, then stopping, released her sight, and she found herself in a spacious gothic room, from whence the men withdrew, leaving her to the care of a female attendant.

She threw herself into a chair, and besought the interposition of the Almighty in her favour.

"Look down, oh heaven!" she cried, "upon an injured helpless female, who has no hope of succour but from thy all gracious hand!"

Having paused a while, her beauteous countenance clouded with grief, she addressed the woman.

"For mercy's sake!" she exclaimed, "tell me where I am, and for what detained?"

"Dear lady," replied Alice, so was the attendant called, "do not ask me, I must not satisfy you; my Lord Fitzallan would never forgive me, was I to disclose one circumstance that he wishes concealed. To be sure this castle belongs to him, and he has been in love with you for a long time: he employed Stephen in the business, who personated a Knight to impose on you, and your father. In sooth, I cannot say much in his favour, for making himself a party in such a black affair; for black it certainly was: he intended to pass a sham marriage on you, and would then have resigned you to his master. I have been intrusted in the whole affair, because they knew my fidelity and secresy was to be relied on: nevertheless, I cannot approve their doings; but I am resolved to keep my opinion to myself for all that."

"Well," said Emma, assuming as much feigned composure as she could, "I suppose I am to continue here a prisoner!"

"Indeed I do not know," returned the attendant; "it is the worst thing in the world for a domestick to betray the secrets of her employer. You are not absolutely a prisoner to be sure; though, I believe, you will be locked up here till you consent to what my Lord requires of you."

Emma turned pale.

"Holy virgin!" exclaimed Alice, "what ails you, lady? I am afraid you do not much covet the honor he designs you: I say nothing; he is a good master to be sure, and, notwithstanding, he cut Joseph's head in twain the other day, for not bringing him his helmet when he asked for it; and almost murdered the old porter, for admitting a woman with a petition; yet, I dare say, he will be very tender to you."

"Why you have given me a sufficient proof of the tenderness of his disposition, I confess," quoth Emma.

"Nay, as to the matter of that," replied Alice, "he was in a passion at the time, for which all his servants blame him, and mention his conduct to every one that comes near the castle:

but, for my part, I despise such paltry work: thank my stars! I can hear all, see all, and say nothing: silent as a Turkish mute, or I should not have been so long in my Lord's family. I never blab, never! his bringing damsels here is nothing to me; and, though he does so every week, I would scorn to say as much even to my own sister."

"Gracious heaven," cried Emma, "what will become of me!"

"Nay, do not give way to melancholy neither," returned the waiting maid, "if it is agreeable to you, I will call old Sandy, our minstrel, who is lately come from the north, and he shall play a Scottish air, or dance a Highland fling, or any thing you may please."

"You are very kind," said the fair captive, "but my mind is out of tune, and the harmony you mention would be lost on me."

"Oh, bless you!" quoth Alice, "there is not much harmony in Sandy's bag-pipes, though, for certain, he makes a charming noise with them sometimes. But, madam, as you are not disposed for merriment, suppose you go to bed: for my own part, I am very drowsy, but I would scorn to say so if my eye-strings cracked."

"I will," replied Emma, "and, if I imagined you would not think it intruding on your good nature, I should request you to partake of my couch."

"Why, as to that matter," said the attendant, "I should have no objection, only—only—"

"Only what?" interrogated the fair prisoner.

"Why I have heard strange stories of the next room where you will sleep; they say it is haunted: I would not propagate such a report for the universe; though I believe it is true nevertheless."

"I fear not that," returned Emma, "and if you can insure my safety from the living inhabitants of this place, I shall not be much alarmed at any others. But pray, what reason have you for your assertion?"

"Assertion!" cried Alice, "I do not assert any such thing, I only say it is so: you must know lights are very often seen in that chamber, and no person can tell how they come there. And, indeed, what is it to any body? 'though some people are so fond of the sound of their own tongue, that they will say any thing, rather than be silent. But, indeed, madam, you had better withdraw, it grows very late."

"I will," quoth the afflicted maiden, "for the present, therefore farewell."

She then took a taper, and, unlocking a door which her attendant informed her was that of her apartment, retired for the night, while the grating of the key convinced her she was indeed a captive.

She looked around the room; it was most desolate and dreary; a few sticks were formed into a fire, which was insufficient to dry the chilly damps that trickled down the hangings; the horror of her situation recurred, if possible, with double force.

"Just God," she exclaimed, "if thy all-righteous power permit those souls, that have quitted this their mortal clay, to wander upon earth again, even such a spot as this must be their sad resort. To thee, however, I commend myself; with thy impenetrable shield over-shadow me; and, if it be thy will that I experience the calamities which seem to threaten, endue me, I beseech thee, with fortitude to bear them!"

She now reclined upon her couch; but the aid of renovating sleep, that wished suspension of our earthly cares, fled her pillow. Throughout the night the chilly north wind whistled through her grated window, and shook the tattered tapestry; while from the lofty turrets, the croaking raven, and portentous screech-owl, in dismal concert filled the dusky air.

On Alice tapping at the door in the morning, she arose languid and unrefreshed; and, going to the casement, what was her astonishment, when she beheld from thence the valley, in which she had passed her youth; the habitation in which she first drew her breath, and the bank whereon she had frequently listened to the artless tale of Leonard! Cruel, painful retrospection! How different her present state; captive to a wretch she despised, and possibly never to see her lover more! she knew not at the time, that in the very room where she had spent the night, the object of her tenderness had passed one before!

On quitting the chamber, she was accosted by her attendant, who inquired how she had rested?

"Alas!" returned Emma, "never shall I know rest again!"

"Do not talk in that manner, dear madam," quoth Alice, "my Lord is coming to visit you; he charged me not to utter a word to you about it; and I must acknowledge one thing; notwithstanding what people say of his being so bad a man, which I would not do for the world, nay, not even repeat it, for talebearers are as bad as tale-makers, they say; yet he must at least be a sensible one, by selecting me for his confidential domestick!"

With these words she left the apartment; but had scarce disappeared, when Edmund entered, with all the deep dissimulation in his countenance, of which he was so complete a master.

"Welcome," he said, "thrice welcome to the castle of Fitzallan: since it was founded, never did so bright a trophy, as thy lovely self, enter its walls."

The heart of Emma, like boiling water in a confined vessel, was bursting her breast with indignation.

She replied, "I do not, nor do I wish to understand the purport of this studied compliment: but, I charge thee, tell me for what I am detained? What right hast thou to tear me from my friends, and to confine me in this barbarous manner from those most dear to me?"

"Ah, Emma!" cried Fitzallan, "to love alone impute the offence, if it be one, or to your own bright charms. Long have I struggled with my passion, and sought to drive the urchin from my heart, but all in vain; for even now, thus beauteous as thou standest before me, his arrows doubly pierce me, and I entreat your hand. Consent but to be mine, I will make you mistress of my wide domain, and place thee in a sphere that Princesses would envy."

"For shame, my Lord!" quoth the maiden, "profane not the sacred epithet of love, by bestowing it upon your guilty flame: how poor, how base, how unworthy of the blood you boast, has been your conduct. Think you nobility can sanction villany? No! though with impunity your deeds may pass on earth, yet, be assured, there is a judge with whom your title will not aught avail; where the departed spirit of the indigent shall cry for vengeance on the vicious great; nor cry in vain!"

Fitzallan gazed on her, rivetted with admiration to the spot, such is the power of virtue; till awaking from his reverie; "No more of this dull stuff," he said, "which sordid Monks preach to the doating part of human-kind, to rob them of their gold; but oh! speak kindly to me."

"Never!" replied Emma; "here, before that Deity you have so much offended, I solemnly declare I never will be your's; but pine my life, if such must be the alternative, in this gloomy dungeon!"

"Indeed! Is it even so?" exclaimed Edmund, irritated at her indifference; "I know full well for whom I am thus scorned; the beggar Leonard has your heart; I, however, have your person; let then your love-sick swain tune his discordant pipe amidst surrounding branches, or beside some flowing rill; I will feast myself on more substantial joys. You are in my grasp, remember, nor all the earthly, all the heavenly powers, shall tear you from me."

"Can you think so meanly of me," she cried, "as to suppose your threats can terrify me into what my heart abhors? My innocence, like the solid rock that braves the billows, is proof against your menaces and arts, and alike despises your frothy eloquence and malice."

With fury in his looks, Fitzallan now darted from the room, and left the afflicted Emma to her sorrows. Long, however, she was not permitted the sad consolation of venting her grief in private, as Alice presently made her appearance.

"In the name of the blessed virgin!" she said, "what possesses my Lord? I never saw him in such a passion before: he raves like a madman; swears you shall be his, let the consequence be what it may: and, as that is the case, you had better be so in an honest way if you can, you know."

The injured maiden returned no answer to her attendant's advice; indeed, she hardly heard it. Frequently she was persecuted by the addresses of Edmund, who visited her daily, but to no purpose; her vows were pledged to Leonard, and she shuddered even at the thought of breaking her plighted faith.

The talkative, and facetious Alice, was her constant companion, and strove to cheer the drooping spirits of her prisoner.

As on the first morning, so she continued to knock at the chamber door of Emma, at the usual hour of rising. One day, however, no answer was given; she tapped again, and again all was silent; she then unlocked the portal, and went in, but the apartment was void; the mark where Emma had thrown herself upon the bed, was the only vestige that remained. Terrified, she descended to the kitchen, and informed the domesticks the young lady was gone.

"Gone!" quoth one, "How? Where was she kept?"

"In the *Black Tower*," said Alice, "and I am sure the ghost has taken her away."

"Peace!" cried Gregory the steward, in a peremptory tone, "or you shall rest there to-night, and then, perhaps, the *ghost* will carry you away; let me advise you to restrain your speech, or, by the blessed crucifix! there will I confine you."

"No, for heaven's sake, good master steward, don't lock me up there: believe me I was ignorant that the ghost," (Gregory frowned,) "I mean the gentleman, that they say lives in the *Black Tower,* was a friend of your's, or I would have sooner died, than mentioned him with disrespect."

"Silence!" exclaimed the steward, "once more let me counsel you to keep a curb upon your tongue, or ——"

"You will clap a padlock upon it, I suppose."

"This is too much," cried Gregory, "Peace, I command you!"

Alice promised obedience, and kept her word; the terror of the *Black Tower* did more than the idea of any human power— it silenced her.

CHAPTER II

The gaudy, blabbing, and remorseful day
Is crept into the bosom of the sea;
And now loud howling wolves arouse the jades
That drag the tragic melancholy night;
Who, with their drowsy, slow, and flagging wings,
Clip dead mens graves, and, from their misty jaws,
Breathe foul contagious darkness in the air.

SHAKESPEARE.

——'Tis dreadful!
How rev'rend is the face of this tall pile,
Whose ancient pillars rear their marble heads,
To bear aloft it's arch'd and pondrous roof!
By its own weight made stedfast, and immoveable.
Looking tranquillity, it strikes an awe
And terror to my aking sight! The tombs
And monumental caves of death look cold,
And shoot a chilness to my trembling heart.

CONGREVE.

IT is now proper to make mention of the means by which Leonard had escaped from the dungeon, wherein he had been so unjustly confined. On the day preceding the death of the wretched Gertrude, she entered his prison, and liberated him; at the same time saying, "She would, in a short time, give him a strong proof of her affection, when she hoped to find him less indifferent."

The Knight hardly made her an answer, but, with Owen, sallied from the castle in quest of his adored mistress. Long, very long, did he continue his search; about half the Isle of Albion did he traverse, but without effect; no trace, or clue, could he obtain to guide him.

One evening, just as they entered on a dreary heath, the dismal aspect of the clouds foretold an approaching storm, which speedily followed its melancholy harbinger: big thunder

103

rattled over their heads; and shook the earth even to its foundation; sulphurous flames flashed, at intervals, across the glade, and disclosed the horrors of the dreary landscape.

Leonard looked round for some place where they might gain a shelter from the rain, which now poured down in torrents.

"Good Heavens!" cried Owen, "What have I done, that I am so severely punished? Oh! if ever I am so happy as to see my poor old father and mother, adieu to all adventures!"

"Peace!" interrupted his master, "Must I be always employed in correcting you for cowardice?"

"Why really," quoth the 'Squire, "if you continue these excursions, I am afraid you will. *By the valour of my Ancestors!* A man had need have as many lives as a cat, that follows the trade of a Knight-errant.

Again his master commanded silence, and proceeded on his course; but had not rode far, 'ere he was startled by his follower, who vociferated, "A reprieve! a reprieve!"

Leonard, who was unused to any exclamation of joy upon these occasions from Owen, inquired the cause.

"Oh! I have cause enough," replied he, "only look to your left."

The Knight did so, and beholding a glimmering light at some distance, spurred towards it. On his near approach he found it proceeded from the window of a gothic mansion, which he judged to have been a monastery, but was almost fallen to decay: large fragments of the ruin, covered with moss, and half buried in the ground, were scattered about: a number of old elm trees, through whose foliage the wind sighed with a melancholy sound, cast a deep shade upon the dreary pile; and the ivyed battlements were now the receptacle of the airy carrion, whose hoarse notes swelled the rumbling storm.

Leonard knew not whether to proceed or retire; Owen advised the latter, which he himself considered most prudent; but thinking he might possibly gain some refreshment, of which they were in great need, he resolved to venture. Unsheathing his sword, therefore, and recommending himself to the divine protection, he boldly advanced; while his courageous 'Squire, who shook as though he had had an ague, reluctantly followed, saying, *"By the valour of my ancestors!* it is all over with us!"

They now entered the gate, which conducted them into a spacious court-yard, over grown with weeds; there they fastened their steeds, and from thence gained the chapel.

"For the love of mercy, sir!" quoth Owen, who could no longer conceal his fears, "do not go any farther; my courage is leaving me!"

"Silence," cried his master, "and, if you are afraid to accompany me, tarry where you are."

"I will," replied Owen, "and now, Saint David and Saint George, if you are the good natured gentlemen we are taught to believe, get me out of this infernal place, and do what you please with me."

Meanwhile the Knight perceived, by a faint beam of moonlight which darted through the painted casements, a stair-case; determined to discover where it led to, he instantly ascended, and, having gained the summit, found himself in a narrow passage, through which, with much difficulty, he made his way; but had not far advanced, 'ere he received a violent blow upon the cheek; and, at the same time, a mournful wind howled through the various avenues of the monastery. He started with terror; big drops of sweat stood on his temple; his knees in violent agitation smote their fellow, and he rushed forward in all the horror of despair; till, turning a corner of the passage, he perceived a faint light stream from the gloom; he approached, and found it came from a spacious room, the folding doors of which were ajar; he entered; a small taper stood upon a table in the midst of the chamber, but gave so insufficient a light, that one end was wrapt in palpable darkness, and the other scarce broke in upon by a faint beam, that streamed through a large window covered with ivy. The wainscot, of oak, had originally been hung with tapestry, several vestiges of which still clung to it, and the various costly reliques of paintings, and their decorations, gave indisputable evidence of the former grandeur of the place. The dying embers of a recent fire, threw a sickly gleam; and on the floor were scattered remnants of viands, and half empty flasks of wine.

Weak and exhausted, this was a cheering sight, and he availed himself thereof; then, taking the taper, he left the apartment. On going out at the door, he observed another passage to the left, which he resolved to explore; it was long, and terminated in a kind of consistory, the boards of which appeared loose; and, 'ere he had taken three steps thereon, the floor gave way with him, and he fell through it.

He arose with much difficulty, and violently stunned, although, fortunately, the spot whereon he dropped, was covered with a quantity of soft earth, that yielded to his weight. He now found himself in a spacious vault, arched in the gothic manner; several large ramified windows in it, and supported by six massy pillars, down whose sides the damp moisture trickled in pigmy rivulets.

Leonard now sought to regain his sword, which, in his fall, he had lost; and, searching the ground with his fingers, he laid hold of the body of a man, clammy and putrid. He trembled with horror; his hair stood erect, and his brains grew cold within his head.

A blast of wind now rushed through the vault, and a massy iron door, that grated on its hinges, slowly opening, presented to his eye a broken stair-case, down which streamed a blue and paly light.

Appalled, Leonard, spite of his resolution, was almost annihilated by surprise and terror; he knelt down, and prayed fervently to that power from whom alone he could expect relief: then, finding himself more calm, he again began to search for his falchion, when a moon-beam falling on the blade, at once restored it to its owner.

He ascended the stairs, at the head of which was a door with a large grate, whence exhaled the light that had attracted his attention. He paused—ardent curiosity prompted him to look through the iron-work—he did so, but, oh God! — — — — — — — — — — what a spectacle for a lover presented itself!—Emma, his loved Emma, sat within! her cheek reclined upon her hand, and pearly drops of woe trickling down her face.

Leonard's frame was agitated by grief and anger, and he called upon her name; on which the maid uttered an exclamation of surprise, and sunk into a swoon.

The Knight was now doubly distressed; he gave way to all the transports of ungoverned fury, and descended, in hopes of finding some weapon with which he might burst the envious door that separated them. On re-entering the vault, he flew to the window, and, with Alcides' force, wrenched one of the bars that secured it, with which he again repaired to his mistress's dungeon, and, sought to gain admission, but in vain; it braved his utmost efforts, and he ceased, weary, exhausted, and hopeless of restoring her to liberty: pausing awhile, again he undertook the arduous task, and with more success; the portal, after a long resistance, yielded, and he caught Emma in his arms!

They now prepared to depart, and had just quitted the dungeon, when the sound of foot-steps, fast advancing, vibrated on their ears; and, in the same instant, an armed man appeared upon the stairs, who recoiled at seeing the son of Christopher; but recovering himself, he rushed forward, telling him to be upon his guard, when, in the stranger's voice, the Knight recognized that of Fitzallan.

A fierce combat, sustained on either side with valour, now took place, until the falchion of Leonard piercing the side of his antagonist, gave a passage for his foul soul to quit its body. Just at this period, they observed another person advancing, who, on viewing Edmund prostrate on the ground, precipitately withdrew, and in a moment vanished from their sight.

CHAPTER III

Ay, but to die, and go we know not where;
To lie in cold obstruction, and to rot;
This sensible warm motion to become
A kneaded clod; and the delighted spirit
To bathe in fiery floods, or to reside
In thrilling regions of thick ribbed ice;
To be imprison'd in the viewless winds,
And blown with restless violence round about
The pendant world, or to be worse than worst
Of those, that lawless and incertain thoughts
Imagine howling! 'tis too horrible!
The weariest and most loathed worldly life
That age, ache, penury, imprisonment,
Can lay on nature, is a paradise
To what we fear of death.
                                        SHAKESPEARE.

ON perceiving the blood fast-flowing from Fitzallan's side, Leonard's anger dissolved, like snow before the rays of the sun; and the softer dictates of pity entering his breast, he flew to the assistance of his antagonist, and endeavoured to staunch the wound, from which the purple stream of life rushed with impetuous course.

"Your unmerited care," quoth the expiring Edmund, "is vain, and tears my mind, worse than your falchion's edge my mangled body. To that from which I came I now return, and oh! I would to heaven my crimes might end with me! but that is hopeless; too sure there is a God, whose delight it is to punish those that have dared to violate the sacred precepts of religion, and who will hurl me to the deep bottom of everlasting flames."

"Think not too hardy of futurity," said Leonard, "nor fear but the Omnipotent is far too merciful to chastise those, who, by repentance, seek to atone their failings."

108

"Alas!" replied Fitzallan, "Do you suppose the penitence of a wretch, that in a few short moments will be nothing, can expiate the complication of enormities I have committed? I dare not even hope forgiveness: attend, however, I beseech you to [hear] my confession, for sure a darker scene of villany was never revealed to wondering mankind, than that which clogs my bosom!

"The late Lord Fitzallan, my cousin, the best of friends and men, married a woman, the amiable counter-part of himself, with whom he lived a few short years in perfect happiness; till, by his invitation, I went to pass some time with them in North-umberland, when my heart was instantly caught by the beauty of his consort: an incestuous passion fired me, and vainly were the barriers of reason, and of conscience, opposed against its resistless force. I determined some way to make her mine; and sure the blackest thought that ever invaded the human breast, then entered mine. I formed the horrid resolution of murder-ing my cousin! the man whose lavish friendship made me what I was!

"I endeavoured to convince myself it would be acting justly; a thousand ideas, that never before had struck me, now pre-sented themselves. I accused fortune for bestowing on him what I strove to consider my right. Thus, instead of flying from the Syren, who first seduced my heart from rectitude, I drank the fatal poison, and sought an antidote in blood.

"Having prepared two ruffians, and given them their orders, I enticed my unsuspecting cousin from the castle, and making our peregrination long, contrived not to return till twilight; then proposed our walking homeward by the clift. We did so, and, passing by its eastern point, which you remember is over-grown with lofty oaks, suddenly my bravoes issued from the thicket, and attacked him: he defended himself with valour, and doubtless would have been victorious, which I observing, drew my sword, and plunged it in his body! he turned, cast a look of mournful reproach at me, and, like great Cæsar, when the blade of his loved Brutus pierced him, with a deep sigh he died!

"Wretch as I was, the arrows of compunction reached my heart, and I would willingly have resigned my life, could I but have restored him. My repentance, however, was but short; and my next consideration was, how to dispose of the corpse. One of the villains was for casting it into the sea; but I, more wary than my colleague, recollected the tide might throw it on the sands, and thereby discover the execrable deed. They proposed, however, to strip him, and concealing his garments, to disfigure his features, and then commit him to the waves. I consented, and these inhuman wretches having mangled his countenance, that the eye of his widowed wife could not have recognized him, threw him from the precipice.

"I tarried with the bravoes till it was dark, then returned to the castle, and, entering it privately, retired to a remote part with the gory habiliments, and deposited them in a small closet, which no one, save my cousin, who had shewn it to me, was acquainted with; then smoothing my features, I repaired to the apartment of Arthur's consort.

"She was setting in much agitation for the unusual absence of her lord, concerning whom she questioned me. I begged her to be silent on that subject, and to consider me henceforward by that name. These words I was about to accompany with a warm embrace, but she repulsed me."

"Villain," she cried, "tell me, I charge thee, where is thy cousin?"

"Spite of my fixed resolve not to be trifled with, I shrunk abashed; my warm circling blood stood, like the stagnate pool, cold, and unmoving, in my veins, and my courage, as the black mist of night disperses at the chearful sight of day, evaporated.

"I faintly answered I knew not; but from the agitation of my frame, and my abrupt declaration, she judged the worst."

"Wretch!" she exclaimed, "produce my husband, or dread the vengeance of an enraged woman!"

"She arose from her seat, and was about to call her people, which I observing, seized her arm, and fastened the door.

"It is to no purpose, I said, your giving way to grief, or anger; they are alike impotent: they neither can recall the dead, nor inflict the vengeance you have threatened on the living.

"I was about to proceed, but the certainty of her Lord's fate banished the spark of hope that had glimmered in her heart, and left her a prey to dire conviction; she sunk supine upon the ground, and I, thinking this a fit opportunity to remove her where her cries would not be heard, conveyed her to the *Black Tower;* then carrying thither her two infants, I left them in custody of one of my myrmidons, and retired; but not to rest; conscience, the bane of sleep, haunted my pillow; nor had I closed my eyes, when the first tints of morn broke in upon my window. I then arose, and went to the apartment of my wronged prisoners. But how can I describe my rage, and disappointment, on finding it empty?

"I instantly summoned my blood-hounds, but only one appeared, the man who has since attended me as my 'Squire; the other was no where to be found. I was almost frantic at this intelligence, and my timid soul surmised that they were gone to lay the case before my king. This idea harassed me, and kept my tortured fancy in a continued ruffle. I found it necessary, however, to do more than sit quietly beneath my apprehensions; I therefore collected the domesticks, and informed them my fears were grievous on my cousin's account, who had not been at the castle on the preceding night; that his lady had absconded, which prompted me to suspect she was at the bottom of the mystery wherein his fate was wrapped: that, if so, she had doubtless art to carry her schemes to greater lengths, and possibly we might be all involved in ruin. I therefore conjured them to consider me as an unworthy substitute for their Lord, assuring them they would find me fully as indulgent; and concluded by saying, I hoped, should any force be used against the castle, they would defend it to their utmost power. In short, so plausible was my tale; so fraught with art; and I forced my crocodile tears so plentifully down my face, that every one of them vowed they would die for me, and departed the room, calling for vengeance on their innocent mistress.

"Thus did I triumph in my villany; but fear, the shadow of crimes like mine, still disturbed me, and never did I close my eyes, but I dreamed the officers of justice were entering to apprehend me, or that I was suffering the severest agonies of offended law. I racked my brain for a remedy, and, at last, the idea of digging a subterraneous passage occurred.

"I remained tortured by anxiety for the space of two years, when I was summoned by the King to court. I obeyed reluctantly, and, fearful the horrid deed had transpired, scarce dared to meet my Sovereign's eye. He, however, quickly dissipated my uneasiness; condoled with me on my cousin's mysterious absence; and invested me as lawful heir, with all his wide domains: from that period I resided at my paternal castle in the west of England.

"At times, I used privately to visit my estate, unknown to any of the inhabitants, save my Steward, Gregory, who was in the secret. On these occasions I used to enter the apartment in the *Black Tower*, by means of the subterraneous entrance; and, form the light which then issued from the same, the superstitious constitutions of the peasantry concluded it was haunted. In that room you slept, by my order, and Stephen, through the passage I have mentioned, entered it. Providentially you were not on your couch, or your life had sure been lost. You escaped; but during my 'Squire's sojourn in the valley, he saw your beauteous, virtuous mistress, and the description he gave, inspired me with love and revenge. I instantly, therefore, made him assume the character of a Knight, and, under that disguise, he offered Emma's father to receive her hand, letting him know his pretended wealth.

"The most virtuous of mankind may be lured by gold, and the old man swallowed the gaudy bait; while his daughter not only refused, but fled the place. My trusty emissary, however, traced her to the Isle of Wight, and, by my command, bore her from thence to the castle in the valley, where she remained till I received intimation you were arrived in England; and, fearing you might discover her abode, I removed her to this ruinous monastery, which is now the receptacle of a banditti, who, partly by bribes, and fear, are under my subjection. At the same time, hardened as has been my nature, I feel a satisfaction in telling you, she returns to you chaste as when you left her.

"One thing moreover learn of me, that the ruffians who attacked you in the wood, and, but for the timely interposition of the noble Edgar, had destroyed you, were but the agents of my envy and revenge; unused to be overthrown, I could not bear the reflection of your having vanquished me, and employed those wretches to dispatch you, for which I now ardently supplicate forgiveness."

Leonard having assured him of his pardon; "I thank you," said Fitzallan (then starting, as though horror struck) "Ha!" continued he, "tell me, I entreat, now while I have breath to ask, whose portrait is that you wear around your neck?"

"I know not," said Leonard, "it was given me by my father, with a strict charge never to lose, or part with it: he moreover said, my future happiness depends upon it."

"Indeed!" cried Edmund, "then there are gods whose care it is to reward the innocent, and punish the guilty! Learn of me, thou art not the offspring of the rustic Christopher—noble blood flows in thy veins—thou art——"

Nature could no more; the glass of life was drained, and he expired, leaving Leonard in a state of uncertainty!

CHAPTER IV

Night, thou foule mother of annoyance sad,
Sister of heavy death, and nurse of woe,
Which wast begot in heaven, but for thy bad
And brutish shape, thrust downe to hell below,
Where, by the grim floud of Cocytus flowe,
    That dwelling is Herebus' black hous,
(Black Herebus, thy husband, is the foe
    Of all the Gods) where thou ungracious,
Half of thy days doest lead in horrour nedeous.

SPENSER.

WHEN Edmund breathed no more, the lovers were at a loss how to act; unjustly as he had treated them, Leonard could not bear the idea of leaving his body divested of the common rites of burial. The great law of human nature, however, self-preservation, aided by the fears of his fair companion, predominated, and they quitted this scene of death.

Passing through the chapel, Emma vented a loud shriek, and recoiled with terror. The Knight inquired the cause of her alarm; without answering, she pointed to a monument, upon which the moon darted her watery beams, and discovered part of a man's head. Leonard, advancing to the place, found his mistress's fears were roused by Owen, who, in his panic, had concealed himself behind the sepulchre, and was nearly as stiff, and inanimate, as the clay which it contained.

"Come forth!" cried his master, "thou disgrace to manhood; Come forth, I say!"

"Do not talk, sir! do not talk!" muttered the woful 'Squire, whose teeth chattered, "but down upon your marrow bones, and call upon the saints to relieve us! Would you believe it, it is not long ago since I saw my old enemy Stephen run across the hall; and, *By the valour of my Ancestors!* I am sure there must be devils in this place, or he would not have been here! Why

114

my great grandfather, Lewellyn, when he was driven amongst the Welch mountains, never underwent more than I have done! Holy Virgin! bless and protect me from all hobgobblins, say I."

Leonard, unmindful of this exclamation, hurried to the court-yard, where, having mounted, they fled across the heath, as the active stag bounds over the lawn when followed by the deep yelling pack that seek his life. Emma's apprehensions were so powerful, it was with difficulty her anxious lover could support her; in every murmur of the breeze she fancied she could distinguish the voices of men: her fears, too, were greatly exaggerated by the cowardice of Owen, who could hardly keep his seat. The son of Christopher upheld her sinking spirits, while the 'Squire, at every other step, turned his head back toward the building they had just quitted; and suddenly, with a tremor on his voice, requested his master to halt; then desired him to cast his eyes upon the monastery: he did so, and beheld numberless lights from the windows of the gothic fabric, and shortly after torches issue from the gate, which swiftly moved in different directions about the dreary heath, casting a dreadful gleam around, and adding to the horrors of the night, which was most dark and dismal.

The Knight immediately clapped spurs to his steed, and again pursued his course, with all the fleetness he possessed. The lights, however, approached, and he found his pursuers gained upon him. Careless about his own safety, but anxious, even to distraction, about his fair mistress, he knew not how to act. To stay, and combat superior numbers, were sure to lose her, and escape was hopeless.

His mind was harassed by these reflections, when he dis-covered a beaten track to the right, and as soon resolved to follow it; having rode about a mile, he paused, and, looking towards the road he had just quitted, had the happiness to find the banditti, (for it was them) had taken another course.

Emma, whose apprehensions had hitherto sustained her feeble frame, found, with the danger, her strength evaporate, and, at length, she sunk into a swoon. Leonard instantly consigned her to the care of Owen, and sallied forth in quest of some water to restore her; commanding his 'Squire to tarry in the place where he left him.

The night was wrapped in an indiscriminate darkness, and he traversed the forest for some time, but could discover no spring to supply his wants; when, as he was about to abandon his search, the welcome murmur of a water-fall broke through the stillness that reigned around. He approached, and having filled his helmet, returned to the spot where he had left his fellow travellers, but it was void, nor did any vestige remain to inform him which way he should bend his steps in quest of them. He called upon his Emma's name, in a voice of distraction; no answer, however, was received, save by the moping owl, and rustling foliage, which, as in concord with his own feelings, trembled in the blast.

When he had partly shaken off the stupefaction wherein surprise and vexation had enveloped him, he racked his brain in conjecturing whither they had vanished: after a torturing interval, it occurred to him, that the banditti might possibly have overtaken, and captured them, during his absence. This idea was no sooner formed, than confirmed: to the monastery he determined to repair, and release his mistress, or perish in the attempt.

With infinite difficulty he retraced the road he had so lately passed: but, alas! how different his sensations! then in possession of what he held most dear on earth; now (like the merchant, who, on the beach, viewing his richly laden vessel, at the moment he thinks himself secure of the wished treasure, is, by the envious rocks and billows, robbed of her for ever,) deprived of what he prized beyond his life.

At length, however, he gained the monastery; and, having fastened his steed to a loose fragment of stone, whereof divers were scattered around, he entered the court-yard, which was filled with horses; these he knew belonged to the banditti; and he rushed forward in the fond hope of finding his lost Emma.

He crossed the chapel, and ascended the staircase, when his ears were invaded by the voices of several people, who appeared in deep discourse. They issued from the apartment before him, and which was the same wherein he had regaled himself. With cautious steps he approached the door, which was not quite closed, and beheld a large group of men therein, and, in the midst of them he discovered Emma. He paused, and heard the following dialogue:

"'Tis all in vain," said one of the banditti, for so they were, "your seeking to deceive us; you may as well walk through the stone walls of the monastery, as hope to do it: no, no, we understand our trade better than to be overshot by you."

"True," quoth another, "and therefore, my dainty damsel, you had as good confess the truth; and who, besides the cowardly dog we took with you, assisted in the murder of Lord Fitzallan; for I should as soon expect a gnat to sting a lion to death, as that dastard to overcome a man."

"Besides," cried a third, "we shall stand a severe rebuff from our captain, when he hears of my Lord's death."

"No," replied the second robber, "the sight of this delicious morsel will cool his anger: how happy will he be to have her in his power."

"You are mistaken," exclaimed the man that first spoke, "I was the person that saw her, and was the means of her being retaken; and, as the Lord Fitzallan cannot *conveniently* come to claim her, I shall not tamely give up my right to our commander, Guy. I am not one of those fools that like to sow, and let others reap the fruit of their labour. However, I am not of a covetous disposition, and we will e'en share alike; so let us all round give her a hearty smack: Come, I will begin."

At these words he approached his timid prey, and was about to encircle her with his rude arms, when Leonard, who could no longer restrain his rage, rushed into the room, and, with a blow from his keen falchion, prevented his purpose, and laid the ruffian insensate on the floor.

In an instant the Knight was surrounded. What could courage effect against such superior numbers? He was disarmed; and, by this time, the prostrate robber having recovered from the blow, which falling on his casque, had only stunned him, now bitterly upbraided him, accusing him with the murder of Fitzallan, and threatening him with death, for the attack the bravo had himself sustained.

"Can'st thou," he concluded, "deny the charge?"

"I do not," replied Leonard, "I slew him in my own defence, and to right the cause of injured virtue. I would also, but for the interference of this thy crew, have sent thee after him. Hearest thou my confession? Now put your boasted threats in execution; but spare yon guiltless female; savage as you are, revere her sex, and let your vengeance fall on me alone: if thou hast no dread at thus offending the Deity, I have no fear in meeting your malicious revenge."

"Indeed!" exclaimed the robber, "we will put your courage to the test.—This moment is your last."

He unsheathed his sword, and his arm was upraised to strike the fatal blow, — — — — — — — — — — when a man of noble deportment rushed into the room, and commanded the ruffian to with-hold his hand. This, with a growl, was obeyed.

"What!" cried the captain, for so he was, "What can have impelled thee to lift thy weapon against the breast of one disarmed?"

"Why, he lifted his weapon against me when he was armed, and I was determined not to remain in his debt."

"Explain thyself!" said Guy.

"I will," replied the villain, "that fellow, whose part you take, has this very night slain the Lord Fitzallan: nay, never start, by holy Paul 'tis true! You know that damsel I suppose," pointing to Emma, who had fainted, "he ran away with her, spite of bolts, bars, and locks: but we coming home, and discovering their handy work, went after them, and soon found my lady and one of her accomplices. We brought them back, confined her companion, and I, not meaning any harm, was about to give her a *chaste* embrace, when that miscreant rushed suddenly into the room, and felled me, like an ox, to the ground."

"Cowardly villain!" exclaimed Guy, "revengeful monster! in whose bosom not the faintest spark of honour, or generosity, glows, how have you dared to violate my orders? How often have I commanded you, on pain of death, to shed no blood but what necessity compelled? Yet wantonly you were about to take the life of a fellow-creature, and that too, when he had no means of opposing thy dastardly intent."

"It is a pity," returned the culprit, surlily, "that one, so well qualified for the church, should have the command of such a noble set of fellows: we had best all turn Friars, and convert our habitation to its original purpose."

"Ha!" cried the captain, "Do you murmur, reptile? Hence from my sight, and be thankful that your existence does not pay the forfeit of your villany. Release your prisoner instantly," continued he to his men; then addressing himself to Leonard, "Tell me, young man, by what miracle you discovered the dungeon wherein yon female was immured?"

The Knight, having by this time recovered Emma, complied with his request, and related every circumstance most veritably. At the conclusion, Guy declared his joy at the demise of Ed-

119

mund. "You will doubtless," quoth he, "marvel to hear me exult that the wretch is no more: but be assured, though fatally forced to aid him in his crimes, my heart has strenuously abhorred him. He knew each circumstance of this our band, and often threatened, did I not abet his vile enormities, to give us up to the rigorous law. What could I do? Think not so despicably of me, as to suppose fear for my own safety, caused me to assent; but for these my gallant comrades. Alas! my life has been so imbittered by the chalice of misfortune, that I would chearfully resign it.—But to return to yourself; you are free, you, and your lovely mistress; oblige me only by taking a slight repast, and by tarrying until morn, when the gates shall be open to you."

Leonard accepted this kindly invitation without fear or distrust; there was an open candour marked the features of his host, that expelled suspicion, and imperceptibly gained the friendship of his beholders: besides, he had declared himself unhappy, which alone was sufficient to claim the interest of our Knight.

Just as supper was produced, Owen, who was now liberated, entered the room; and, on seeing his master, capered for joy like a mad-man.

"Heaven be praised!" said he, "I have at length found you again! What, and a table well larded with provisions? This is a welcome sight. To say sooth, I expected, if ever again I was *brought to table,* to have been served up as a middle dish: for these worthy, good-looking gentlemen, have cooped me up like a bantam fowl, for fattening; and I feared I was destined to satisfy their *noble* and *cannibal-like* appetites."

Without further ceremony, or waiting to be pressed, he seated himself, and attacked the banquet in a vigorous manner, swearing, *By the valour of his Ancestors!* the wine was delicious.

During supper, Leonard attentively observed his host, whose eyes were oft brimful of tears, and whose breast heaved with reiterated sighs. The repast ended, and the followers of Guy withdrawn, the Knight ventured to question him upon the subject.

"Alas!' replied the captain, the drop of sorrow rolling down his manly cheek, "when I behold yourself, and this fair damsel, cruel retrospection pictures the days! days fled for ever! when, blessed with innocence, I sought the hand of Isabel, whose unhappy fate, mingled with my own sad destiny, may prove an useful lesson to mankind, to curb the accused passions of envy and revenge. Listen, if it so please you, and profit by the example."

Leonard bowed assent, and Guy thus commenced his narrative.

CHAPTER V

Were honour to be scann'd by long descent,
From ancestors illustrious, I could vaunt
A lineage of the greatest, and recount,
Among my fathers, names of ancient story,
Heroes and god-like patriots, who subdued
The world by arms and virtue:
But that be their own praise:
Nor will I borrow merit from the dead,
Myself an undeserver.

ROWE.

"AT Seville, a reputed city in the kingdom of Castile, lived Don Pedro de Segovia, a nobleman of birth and fortune. While in his earliest spring of life, 'twas his fortune, in a conflict with the Moors, to retake a post that had been involuntarily forsaken by a young officer of the same rank as himself."

"The praises with which his Sovereign and superiors in the army, honoured him, stung the envious soul of Ramirez, so was the officer called, to the very quick; and he omitted no opportunity of expressing his chagrin and disapprobation; though never in such direct terms, as to give Pedro sufficient cause to resent his conduct; who saw, with contempt, the jealous eye with which he was observed."

"At length the tumult of war found a period, and the olive of peace was planted in Spain; the soldiers quitted the clangour of the tented field, for the wished embraces of their loved mistresses; in whose arms they found an adequate reward for all their toil and danger."

"On Pedro's return to Seville, he formed an intimacy with a grandee, named Don Fernando de Mendoza, one of the richest and most powerful nobles in all Castile; at whose mansion Segovia was almost a constant inmate. But the chief magnet that attracted him thither, was the lovely Ximena, only child of his friend, and the staff of his age."

122

"Pedro beheld, and loved her; on which he implored the assent of Mendoza, who received his suit with joy; but at the same time referred him to his daughter, refusing to bias her choice, in a circumstance, whereon the future happiness of her life depended."

"You have," said he, pressing the hand of Segovia, "you have, my dear Pedro, my consent as freely as you have asked it; you shall also have my wishes for your success with Ximena. More you, with justice, cannot ask, nor can I grant: the will is free as air, and never should be restrained. Seldom do parents reflect, that, while they fondly hope they are compelling their offspring to be happy, they too frequently launch them into a sea of misery, without a compass that may steer them back to the coast of felicity."

"Pedro returned Fernando his fervent thanks, and instantly sought the apartment of Ximena. With a hesitative step he approached the portal, and his trembling hand struck gently upon the door, which was opened by the maiden herself. She retreated, blushed at the sight of him, and her eyes, unconscious why, were cast upon the floor."

"Is the sight of me," quoth Pedro, "offensive? If so, how shall I acquire courage to declare the cause of my intrusion?"

"This added to Ximena's confusion, and she answered not."

"Am I, most adorable woman," he continued, "to understand this silence as a tacit acknowledgement that my fears are true? If so, as the blue lightning strikes the forest oak, will conviction cleave my heart in twain. After gaining sight of my wished haven, must my bark be wrecked?—Pardon, too lovely Ximena, the incoherency of my language; but the idea of having offended you racks my soul. I come a lowly suitor to you."

"Alas! my Lord," returned the artless maid, "What boon can a weak woman grant?"

"Thy love!" exclaimed Segovia, "Nay, never blush, nor turn averted thus thy countenance; for, by the thousand graces that wanton in thy cheek, unalterably my heart is fixed upon thee!"

"He paused."

"Will you," he then continued, "refuse me? Having obtained your noble sire's consent, will you drive from my breast the hope that there resided? Ah! no! sure thy soft bosom cannot contain so loathsome an inmate as is cruelty; 'tis impossible. May I, then, cherish the idea that time will cause you to look with pity on my sufferings, and to reward my love?"

"I know not," answered Ximena, "whether or no it becomes my virgin state, explicitly to declare my sentiments: but, I must frankly own, no force will be laid upon my inclination in obeying the wishes of my father."

"Encouraged by this favourable declaration, Pedro conjured his friend to fix the nuptial day; and Fernando, finding his daughter declared her willingness to become the bride of Segovia, named it; but, in the interim, an accident occured, that had well nigh blighted their schemes of happiness."

"Some few days previous to the intended marriage, a cavalier waited on Pedro, and presented him this billet."

At these words Guy drew from his breast a letter, which he read to his auditors in the following words.

"Whosoever attempts to gain the heart of a woman, already pledged to another, is a villain, and deserves the chastisement of an injured rival. If Don Pedro dare meet the man he has wronged, and try his sword in single combat, probably fortune may not be so propitious, as when she restored to him the post, unwillingly lost by
                              RAMIREZ DE MURCIA."

"You may possibly be surprised," continued the captain, "that this letter came into my hands; but your wonder will cease, when you are told that I am the son of Don Pedro; my real name Carlos, and that he gave me the billet: but more of that hereafter."

"Indeed!" exclaimed Owen, "Well, you will excuse me, but you must be thirsty, methinks, with talking so long. Come, I'll give you a toast, *Here's to the skull of the donor!*"

The captain knitted his brows, and Leonard commanded silence.

Owen hastily withdrew the cup from his lips, and bowed in token of obedience; on which Carlos, so we shall henceforth call him, continued his discourse.

Unconscious of having, in any wise, offended Ramirez, Pedro demanded an explanation, which the bearer of the letter gave. Saying, "his friend had long made suit to Ximena, and considered his dismission to arise from a preference given to Segovia; who, having promised to attend the challenger on the subsequent day, was left to his own reflections."

Again he perused the letter, the contents of which some-what staggered the confidence he had placed in Ximena's truth: he suspected Ramirez had once held a place in her heart, from whence himself had expelled him. If so, might not some lucky rival retaliate upon him? And, at best, was the heart of such a woman, if such she proved, worth his desiring to keep? Again, he accused himself for doubting her fidelity, which, spite of his utmost efforts to the contrary, he did. Resolved to be no longer racked by suspense, he hastened to the castle of Mendoza, and instantly sought the chamber of his mistress, who received him with her accustomed tenderness, and expressed much uneasi-ness at the agitation visible in his countenance.

The slightest web that ever spider wove, will draw a faithful lover back to his duty: and Pedro was on the point of forgetting the purport of his visit; when, collecting all his firmness, and calling to mind that it behoved him, instead of giving way to an unmanly tenderness, to probe the matter to the quick; he, in the course of conversation, as if casually, mentioned the name of Ramirez; at the same time fixing his eyes steadily on her face; but no trace of guilt could he discover there: virtue and candour adorned the pages of her heart, to which the former was an index.

Pedro now bade adieu to distrust, and resolved to support his claim to her, in defiance of every rival that might oppose him.

On the subsequent day he met Ramirez, who received him with every mark of resentment. "Come, sir," said he, "I tarried for you, let us now decide who is to bear away the fleece for which we do contend: but this remember, or one, or both of us must fall; I am here fixed on losing my own life, or of taking thine: therefore reflect 'ere 'tis too late."

"Would'st thou," returned Segovia, nettled to the quick, "drive me from the field, by telling me of the danger I must face? Oft hast thou viewed this arm scoring the swarthy heads of infidels. Didst ever see me turn my back upon an enemy? No. What is there so appalling in the name of Murcia, then, that I should use reflection 'ere I encounter him?"

"Enough," exclaimed Ramirez, "curse on this woman's war!—Defend yourself!"

"They then attacked each other, and, for a while, conquest hung doubtful in the scale; but the furious passes made by Ramirez, void of all rule, gave his adversary the advantage; whose sword entered his breast, and he fell, incarnading the earth around him."

"Pedro offered his assistance; but the friend who accompanied him, painted, in such strong colours, the danger that awaited him, should Ramirez expire (which indeed appeared but too probable) that he precipitately withdrew from the field of combat, and remained at the mansion of a kindred, until the issue of Murcia's wound was known."

"For several days he received a favourable account thereof; but, at length, he heard that his antagonist had resigned his breath; conjuring his relatives, on his death-bed, not to pursue the rigour of the law against Don Pedro."

CHAPTER VI

——But oh! what form of prayer can serve my turn?
Forgive me my foul murder!
That cannot be.————

SHAKESPEARE.

SOON after the demise of Ramirez, Don Pedro espoused Ximena: but, though blest with the woman he adored, and basking in the sun-shine of his sovereign's favour, his happiness was not unalloyed. The death of the ill-timed Murcia, cast a thick shade over his prospect of felicity, that greatly diminished it, and he retired from the noise and bustle of the court, to his paternal fields."

"But, 'though withdrawn from the officers of state, he fully discharged the duties of a man. His constant study was to rescue merit from oppression; to oppose unjust power; to reclaim the vicious, and reward the meritorious. Many joyful hearts, over a crackling fire, and a frugal repast, have blest the hand that furnished the means."

"How few are like him? How few endowed with prosperity, consider the debt they owe to Providence? And which they ought to seek to cancel, by dispersing, like the sun his genial rays, their bounty on all around them."

"Pardon this digression, 'tis a tribute to a revered, departed parent."

"My mother, at the time she gave birth to my unhappy self, presented to the world another son. Alphonso, so he was called, was also the brother of my heart; in his society no wish remained ungratified; and in this envied intercourse of mutual friendship and affection did we continue, till we had attained the age of manhood; when the black cloud of fortune was about to pour, from its scowling aspect, the torrent of misery, and to overwhelm us both therein."

"From early infancy the love of arms had fired my breast: with avidity I listened to the battles my father recounted, and longed to imitate the example of the heroes whose names he mentioned. In short, I determined no longer to bury my youth in idleness, but to seek for fame in the field of glory."

"Alphonso wished much to accompany me, but that my parents positively refused."

"No," quoth Don Pedro, "we cannot part with both; Alphonso tarries here with us; but do you, my Carlos, go where honour calls. In the fond hope of again seeing you, we shall endeavour to bear your absence with fortitude. But, rather than your existence should be prolonged at the expence of fame, I would your blood might enrich the scorching sands of Africa. Return, my son, crowned with laurels, or return no more."

"A few days after, (the period fixed for my departure) my father requested me to attend him into the garden, and, with many a sigh, informed me of what I have already recounted, and presented me the letter I have just shewn you."

"I now bade adieu to my paternal mansion, and, attended by a faithful servant of my father's, named Vasquez, and a few other followers, commenced my journey for the Christian camp, and arrived the very day a battle, on which depended the fate of Spain, was about to be decided."

"My heart beat high within me, and I longed for the onset, which soon took place: the brazen cymbols clashed in the air; the hoarse trumpet swelled the gale; and the hollow drum called us to the attack. The Moors, with head-strong zeal, and screams of Alla, rushed furiously on; while the Christians, recommending their cause to their blessed Redeemer, stopped their career, and, at length, forced the infidels to fly before the consecrated banner."

"Several skirmishes afterwards took place; for the Moors were so disheartened, as well as diminished, by their late losses, that they contented themselves with harassing us on every occasion that offered; and, at last, sued for peace: which being granted, our victorious army quitted the field, and, on their return, were welcomed by the acclamations of their countrymen."

"On my journey homeward, I, one evening, stopped to question a cavalier concerning my way to the next town. He informed me, the nearest was a good three leagues from thence, and that, moreover, the road was so bad, he would advise me to tarry till the following day; adding, if I would accept a night's lodging, the doors of his castle were open to me."

"I accepted the invitation, and accompanied him to his mansion, where I was entertained in a manner that fully evinced the hospitality of the owner."

"A fair lady, the daughter of my host, graced the table, and my eyes feasted themselves on her beauties. In the morning I arose, and, with an aching heart, bade them farewell. They kindly pressed me to prolong my visit, and I joyfully caught at the proposal, and remained at the castle, drinking still deeper of the cup of love."

"I had been several days there, when, one stormy evening, in passing the chamber of Isabel, the heavenly accents of her tongue arrested my steps, and I paused at the door."

"Alas!" said she, "ye tempestuous elements! cease your direful conflict: too much do you resemble the war within my breast. Oh Carlos! Carlos!"

"Here her voice seemed to be choked by sighs; I could contain no longer, but, rushing into the room, I threw myself at her feet, and owned my love."

"While in this situation, the chamber door was suddenly opened, and her father appeared at the threshold. He started, frowned, and retired; but, in a few minutes, returned, and, with a solemnity in his manner, requested me to attend him to his closet. I took up a taper, and was about to follow him."

"You need not trouble yourself," quoth he, "to bear a light."

"I set it down again, and attended him to his own room. He threw himself into a chair, and continued for some time buried in reverie; when, seeming to recollect himself, he approached the door, and fastened it, then seated himself, and broke silence in the following terms."

"When I admitted you, an unknown guest, beneath my roof, I little thought you would reward me, by seeking the destruction of my child."——

"He was about to continue his discourse, but I interrupted him."

"My Lord," said I, "banish the thought from your bosom. Most solemnly I swear, holy Maria! hear my prayer! that my passion is pure as white robed innocence! That I love the gentle Isabel 'tis true; and, if I gain your approbation of my passion, I am happy: but rather would I pine my life away in unavailing woe, than repay your kindness with ingratitude."

"Enough," he cried, "But tell me, what sureties have I that thy love is constant; and not of that fickle and airy nature, that every idea of interest will cause to vary?"

"Whatever proof you may demand, my Lord," quoth I, "consistent with the honor of a Spaniard, Saint Jago be my witness! I am ready to give it you."

"Mark me," said he, "Some twenty years ago, then in the prime and heyday of my blood, it was my lot to be enslaved by one, the most lovely, yet cruel of her sex; and the disappointment to view her carried off by an exulting rival, the powers of love, and of revenge, I own, were partly smothered in me; until the situation wherein I found you, blew up the latent sparks, that still lurked in my bosom, into a flame. And, though too late to indulge the former, my soul shall satiate her with revenge. Know, too, this rival lives in peace, and happiness, while I am the victim of misery. Now, mark me well," (continued he, in a low tone, and drawing nearer to me,) "this man I would have dispatched; and you, if that your love is constant as you assert, must be his executioner."

"He paused awhile, and then proceeded."

"Ha! dost hesitate? Nay, thou must, for that way, only, canst thou gain my child: let not, then, the bug-bear, conscience, startle thee, but brace thy manhood to the deed. The name of this accursed rival, who, like a deadly spider crawls in my imagination, and whom I would have brushed from earth, is Pedro de Segovia!——Pierce his very heart; and, when you strike, tell him the blow is to revenge the wrongs of Ramirez de Murcia!"

"A peal of thunder, at that instant, shook the dome; and a flash of lightning exhibited, to me, the features of Ramirez, (for he it was) distorted by rage; while mine were convulsed with horror. There was no time, however, for meditation, as he pressed me for my answer; again reminding me, that on it rested my hopes of Isabel."

"My Lord," replied I, "dearer than life is your fair daughter to me: but even her, and the rich East to boot, I would resign, rather than wade to the possession through a sea of blood."

"'Tis well," he cried, with a sneer, "I knew where your boasted tenderness would end: but, if your love is constant, as you would wish me to think, once more reflect; for, by Saint Jago! on no other terms you have my child."

"My Lord," quoth I, "you have already my determination; nor will you find me waver. How tottering would be the foundation of my happiness, when the base, whereon I reared it, was *parricide!*"

"Ramirez started from his seat, and, in a tone of surprise, reiterated, *parricide!*"

"Yes;" answered I, "in me you behold the offspring of Don Pedro de Segovia: but yet, alas! he is not the happy mortal you have described; the supposition of being your murderer, harrows his feelings, and comfort is a stranger to his bosom."

"Indeed!" cried Murcia, exultingly, "then doth it return to mine: his misery alone is my delight. For thee, instantly quit my castle, or woe upon thy head!"

"Hear me, my Lord, I beseech thee!" replied I, "let not ill-timed revenge cause you to refuse me your fair daughter: consent to give her to me, and let the union heal the breach between our houses."

"Ha! What sayest thou, boy?" exclaimed he, "Dost mean to insult me? Thinkest thou I would condescend to take the hand of him that overthrew me? Never, never will I forgive it! Know, stripling, 'twas by my desire, the report of my death was propagated: and here have I since resided, chewing the bitter cud of retrospection. The world became disgusting to me, from the moment Pedro vanquished me; and my hatred to him, and to his blood, ends only in the grave. But I debase myself, to exchange a word with one sprung from his loins. Instant be gone, nor blast me longer with thy loathed sight!"

"The obduracy of Ramirez dispersed every hope, and I was compelled to depart, without the consolation of even a parting interview with Isabel."

"I mounted my horse, and quitted the castle, with an aching heart. At one of the windows sate my loved mistress; on which I halted, and gazed upon her beauteous face, 'till, actuated by a sudden gust of depression, I clapped spurs to my courser, and, at full speed, departed."

"The agitation of my spirits had so strongly affected me, that a fever ensued almost immediately on my arrival at the castle of Segovia, and, for several weeks, confined me to my couch, and bade defiance to all the skill that the most famed doctors of Seville exerted in my behalf."

"One morn, on awaking, I found Alphonso seated by me; who, taking my hand, thus addressed me."

"Tell me, Carlos, by the affection of our youth, and by every solemn tie, I adjure you, tell me the cause of thy despondency. 'Tis evident thy disease baffles the art of medicine, and, much I fear thy mind is ill at ease."

"Finding I replied not, he thus continued."

132

"Is there ought, my dear brother, I would conceal from thee? Or do you think me unworthy of your confidence, that you trust not to me the cause of thy melancholy? By heaven! I swear, whatever it may be, it never passes my lips!"

"The warmth and affection with which his words were uttered, encouraged me to confess my passion for Isabel. He heard me out, and conjured me to be of comfort; advising me to bear up against my grief, and that, so soon as my strength should be restored, to bear away my mistress, if possible, from the mansion of her unjust father."

"This idea gave me new life, and I mended daily. When perfectly recovered, I again quitted the mansion of my ancestors, never to see it more, attended by the faithful Vasquez, and two other servants, and soon gaining the neighbourhood of Ramirez's castle, took up my abode at a hut, within the distance of a mile from thence."

"When the sun had retired beneath the western horizon, and darkness was diffused over the earth, I used, with anxious step, to walk around the walls that contained my Isabel; and gained a melancholy consolation by gazing on the mansion where she resided."

"One night, alas! while I recount it, wherefore does my heart not crack its cordage? One fatal night, I descried, by the faint beams of the moon, a man lurking beneath the castle walls. I stopped; and, shortly after, saw a female descend from thence, in whose person I recognized that of Isabel!"

"Rage and indignation overcame me; and, calling on the stranger to defend himself, I furiously attacked him: my sword entering his body, he staggered, and I endeavoured to repeat the blow; but the daughter of Ramirez rushing between us, received the point of my falchion in her breast."

"Seeing her fall, I instantly flew to her aid. Santa Maria!" she exclaimed, "Is it my Carlos? Alas! lose not a thought on me, but give assistance to thy generous, wounded brother!"

"I was almost petrified; and, fast as my tottering frame would suffer, approaching the spot where my antagonist laid, discovered the features of Alphonso; his eyes closed in death!"

"Unknowing what I did, I returned to Isabel; who, struggling with mortality, informed me my brother had found means to convey a letter to her, mentioning the method he had planned for her escape, and that he had, that night, contrived to effect his purpose."

"Scarce had she unravelled the mystery of Alphonso's presence there, 'ere she expired, leaving me in a state, bordering on madness."

"Alas!" exclaimed I, "hapless brother, and unfortunate Isabel!—Like the sun shine of an April morn, are our dreams of happiness suddenly lowered by the clouds of mischance! and, as the over-whelming tempest tears the sweet plants of earth from their bed, has my destructive arm beat to the ground the fairest flower of nature!—Just heaven! Are there no bolts, armed with uncommon vengeance, to hurl against the head of such a wretch as I am? A murderer! a fratricide! a monster! unfit to taint the ambient air with my pestiferous breath!"

"My strength here forsook me, and I sunk to the ground, in a state of insensibility. Blessed, happy state! would I had so remained!——But the quiver of misery was not yet exhausted; my breast was destined for its shafts, and miserably have they mangled me!"

"On returning reason, I found myself in the arms of my faithful Vasquez."

"Saint Jago!" he cried, "My worthy young master, what means this dismal scene?"

"It means," returned I, "that you behold a murderer! the butcher of a kind brother, and a faithful mistress!"

"On hearing this, Vasquez approached the body of Alphonso; and, descrying his face, exclaimed, in a tone of wild affright, Oh! horror! horror!"

"This irritated me: I considered it as an infringement on my rights of sorrow, and commanded him to leave me."

"Canst thou, old man," I cried, "shew me thy hand steeped in the precious gore of him that turned with thee? Canst thou proclaim thyself the slaughterer of virgin innocence, or lay thy hand upon thy heart, and say, here is the grand criterion of villany? No. Why then intrude upon my griefs, and strive to mock me with thy puny sorrow? Leave me."

"Good heaven!" cried he, "How little do you know me!—Mock you? It is not in my nature: leave you I cannot."

"Instant be gone," I exclaimed, "or thy blood shall intermingle with the hapless pair before thee!"

"I will not," returned the affectionate creature, "pardon my first act of disobedience; but now I cannot quit you, though death be the alternative. Behold my breast: strike deep your sword: my old veins, though shallow, will pour forth the spring of life; and the last dying accents that hover on my lips, shall bless my master's heir."

"The manner in which his words were uttered, somewhat calmed my rage; but the sense of guilt returned with aggravated force, and, in a paroxysm of despair, I cast myself beside the inanimate bodies."

"My trusty Vasquez, however, fearful I should be discovered in that situation, with the assistance of my two other servants, removed me from this scene of death, and conveyed me in a litter towards my paternal mansion."

"I raved, I supplicated them to release, and suffer me to return to the manes of my slaughtered Alphonso, and Isabel: but deaf were they to my menaces, and entreaties, and bore me to the castle of Don Pedro."

"The distracted state in which I appeared before him, excited his admiration; but when Vasquez informed him of the fatal truth, his grief was only secondary to my own, and redoubled mine: a fever was the consequence, which, for a long period, deprived me of reason. On returning sense, what were my feelings, on beholding the attendants, who surrounded me, in mourning weeds? My foreboding heart presaged the worst; and I questioned them, in vain, for whom they were worn."

"Vasquez, at last, imparted all to me: my father, heartbroken for the loss of Alphonso, had sunk an early victim to the grave; and my mother, the world no longer having any charms for her, had embraced a religious life, and thrown herself within the cloysters of a nunnery."

"To describe my feelings, on receiving this account, would be a fruitless attempt; my passions, 'tis true, were abated, but had sunk into a despondency still more insupportable."

"Having rewarded my servants, and particularly my Vasquez, I bade an eternal adieu to Castile, and sailed for England; every part of the globe being alike indifferent to me."

"Arriving in the neighbourhood of this place, I rested one night at a small house, the abode of a shepherd, who, in the course of conversation, informed me, this monastery was the receptacle of banditti; interlarding his discourse with the various plans exercised by them, to lay the adjacent country under contributions."

"Instantly the thought of enlisting amongst them, flashed, like lightning, across my brain; I considered myself a being, unfit to mix in the society of men, and looked upon these wretches as most proper for me to herd with. I joined them, and was, soon after, elected, by general consent, their chief: yet since my sojourn here, my hand has been guiltless of shedding human blood, and I have strove to allay the savage nature of my comrades."

"I have no friend, no tie, on earth; the world is a wide waste to me; I look forward, with avidity, for the moment when, in the grave, my crimes and memory will, I hope, be buried together."

CHAPTER VII

Eventful day! how hast thou chang'd my state!
Once on the cold, and winter-shaded side
Of a bleak hill, mischance had rooted me,
Never to thrive, child of another soil:
Transplanted now to the gay sunny vale,
Like the green thorn of May, my fortune flowers.

HOME.

HERE the Captain pausing, Leonard and Emma retired to their several apartments for the night; and scarce had the latter dropped into a slumber, when she was awakened by a knocking at her chamber.

Alarmed, she inquired who it was?

"'Tis I, Leonard:" replied a voice in a whisper, "Rise instantly, for even now a plot is forming against our lives. Cursed be the crafty Guy! like silly flies we are entangled in his subtle web. Haste, or we are too late to save ourselves."

Emma equipped herself, and opened the door.

"Extinguish your lamp," said he, in the same low tone, "or it may discover us, and frustrate all our hopes."

She did so, and he led her down a flight of stairs, from whence they gained the courtyard, where they mounted, and proceeded at full speed from the monastery.

They traversed the dreary wild, and, at length, gained a clump of trees.

"Here," said the companion of Emma, "we may repose ourselves, safe from the pursuit of our enemies."

The maiden started; the voice was not that of Leonard, but of a stranger! An universal trepidation seized her, and she scarcely could support her frame, or ask the question she was anxious, yet dreaded, should be solved. At last she summoned resolution to interrogate the stranger, and inquired who he was?

"What!" replied he, "Do you not know me? Is your memory so shallow you cannot recollect your admirer, who, for your sake, had the *honor,* lately, of being stunned by your *true lover's* sword; and, afterwards, the *felicity* to be threatened with death by my commander? However, to convince you I am not the *revengeful savage* Guy talked of, I am about to return good for evil, and favour you with my love: Yes, forgetful of the indignities I have received on your account, I am determined to take you to my arms: so dismount, my fair lady."

Emma used all the eloquence of which she was mistress, to put him from his purpose: but, deaf as the wind, he regarded not her supplications, and tore her from her horse. She then threw herself at his feet, and again besought him to have compassion on her helpless state.

"Why you must think me a pretty fool," quoth he, "to run the risk I have done in making you my prize, and then to give you up: you are a rich booty, and I have hazarded my life to get you; for had my attempt failed, Guy would have taken it without ceremony: however, there is not much fear of him now, for, thank heaven, he is——"

"Here!" exclaimed a voice in thunder; when the villain, turning round, beheld, by the grey twilight, that now broke through the thick foliage, his captain rushing furiously towards him!

They attacked each other like ravenous vultures, when, in a short time, the blood of the ravisher ensanguined the plain, and he resigned his breath.

Emma, relieved from her persecutor, was about to return her generous deliverer every acknowledgement, a heart glowing with gratitude could suggest, when Leonard and his 'Squire appeared. Vain would it be to attempt the description of their meeting; to lovers alone must be left the conception of it.

Owen, with fervency, expressed his joy at this her second deliverance.

"By the valour of my Ancestors!" cried he, "but you have had a couple of narrow escapes; and had it not been for my master, this noble captain, and myself, heaven only knows what had become of you!—Perhaps you would have been destined to satisfy their cannibal-like appetites. But now, sir," addressing Carlos, "as you have kindly thumped the breath out of this worthy wight's body, pray have the goodness to exalt it on the next tree; you know he was high minded; and let his carcase dangle like a bunch of ripe grapes."

"No," quoth the captain, "his life hath made expiation; and to wage war with the deceased, were to degrade the character of a Christian and a man!"

Leonard listened with admiration, and sincerely regreted that one, endued by nature with every sentiment of justice and humanity, should be compelled to link himself with plunderers.

Alas! how fair a page was blotted!

By this time the mist of darkness was dispelled from earth by the sun's burnished rays, and the feathered songsters stretched their little throats towards heaven, and warbled forth their gratitude. The son of Christopher, therefore, prepared to depart. Guy assisted Emma to mount; then, pressing the hand of Leonard, "Farewell," quoth he, "may happiness attend you; may you shun the labyrinth of misery, in which my steps for many a long, long year, have wandered. Think sometimes of the wretched Carlos, who, at one time, would not have disgraced your knowledge; and acquit me, so far, in your good opinion, as to believe not choice, but sad necessity, and a concatination of misfortunes, with which you are acquainted, have made me what I am. Adieu, for ever!"

Leonard cordially thanked him for the kindness he had received from him, and, clapping spurs to his steed, departed.

With light did Owen's courage return, and he began to talk with indifference of the late adventure; swearing, *By the valour of his Ancestors!* he would have peppered their doublets, had they not attacked him unawares.

Another great stimulative to this valorous sally, was the distant view of a village, which, at the same time, whetted his appetite; and he already anticipated the pleasure of attacking some well stored pantry. Having gained the hamlet, they refreshed themselves; and Owen, who allayed his hunger by destroying a venison pasty, accompanied with a flaggon of wine, remounted his horse in high spirits.

They then made for the nearest port, where they hired a small vessel to convey them to the Isle of Wight, resolving to claim the hospitality of Montmorenci: suffice it to say, they landed there, and that the Knight could not refrain from stopping at the cottage of the fisherman.

Peter, on seeing them, forgot his age, and leaped for joy.

"Heaven bless your honour!" he said, "What you have found your little frigate, I see: well, shiver my timbers! I no more expected to set eyes on you again, than I do to be made high Admiral of England! I thought all along," (addressing himself to Emma,) "keel haul me if I did not, that you could not be looking out for a servant's birth, your timbers were so slight: and now it seems, as plain as the mizen, that you were in chace of your lover. But why, instead of laying to, and beating on and off shore, did not you crowd sail, and come in before the wind? I do not think any one would have refused you moorings. And now," turning to the son of Christopher, "let an old tar give you a little advice; when you had this rich cargo under convoy, you had no business to be cruizing on another tack, and leave her adrift."

Leonard smiled at his bluntness, and thanked him for his counsel.

"Nay," replied Peter, "I want no thanks, and I hope your honour will not be offended. You must know, a few days after you set sail from here, I was hailed upon the beach by a milksop, who asked me whether I would let him have my boat for a short voyage, and told me, that I should be handsomely rewarded, and a great deal more of such nonsense: however, he might as well have attempted to sail in the wind's eye, as deceive me in that there way; I paid no more attention to his discourse, than the capstern would have done."

"Avast," cried I, "two words to that bargain; first man the pump of your conscience, and unship a little of your hypocrisy, with which you seem tolerably well freighted: secondly, reef your lingo, and come to the point. What do you want my smack for?"

He said, "to carry off a person who had robbed him in England, and scudded here for harbour."

"I believe you lie! was my answer, for if that is the case, why do not you get proper authority? Where are your sailing orders? Do you think we have not law here, as well as on the other side of the water? Why I believe you are a pirate, and fight under false colours: I wish I had my will of you, d—med but I would tie you up to the gang-way, you lubber, and give you a round dozen in less time than the boatswain could pipe all hands! But, come, shove off, heave a-head, and let me see no more of you, or I will take you in tow to the Baron, and we will hear what he says to you."

The fair weather spark sheared off, like a French ship from an English one, and I never saw him again; but I know, as well as I know stem from stern, he is the booby that captured this here lady."

Leonard admired the rough honesty of the tar, and, taking his leave, repaired to the castle, where his reception surpassed his most sanguine expectation; they greeted him with every mark of hospitality, and were profuse in their congratulations to Emma on her preservation.

A gloom, however, obscured the countenance of the you Knight, that greatly diminished their satisfaction, and at

which his noble host interrogated him. Void of all circumlocu-
tion, he told him every transaction which had occurred during
his absence, concluding with the death of Edmund.

"And although," said he, "the safety of my own life compelled me to the deed; and, notwithstanding mankind must
rejoice that such a monster is cut off from society, I would the
blow had by some other arm been given. His parting words,
moreover, are engraven on the tablets of my memory, and the
mystery attending them has much perplexed me. When the
wretched man had ended his confession, I observed him shud-
der, and he inquired whose picture it was I wore around my
neck? I told him it was given me by my father, with a solemn
injunction to preserve it. Big with some mighty secret, that he
seemed to wish revealed, he faintly struggled with death; but in
vain, the grizzly monarch cut the thread of life, and left me
ignorant of what he wished to say."

During the whole of Leonard's speech, the Lady Montmorenci appeared much agitated; but, at the last sentence, she could
scarce respire.

"Have you the portrait about you?" cried she, gasping for
breath.

"I have," returned the youth.

He presented it to her; and on her perusing the features, she
sunk lifeless upon the floor. All were now busy in reviving her,
which, with infinite difficulty, they effected, and, with returning life, her passion somewhat subsided.

"Heavenly father!" she said, "thy ways are unfathomable!
but let me not give too great a rein to joy. Tell me," she continued, "hast thou the mark of an arrow on thy shoulder?"

"I have," replied the amazed Knight, "and oft, during my
youth, my parents have blessed the mark, and said it was a
proof of the benevolence of Providence that I bore it."

The Baroness could no longer restrain her joy, but rushed
into his arms, exclaiming;

"Receive the blessing of thy mother!"

He dropped upon his knee, while Emma, Julia, and Montmorenci, like statues gazed upon the scene!

Recovering from the first sallies of delight, she addressed her husband.

"Behold, my Lord," said she, "the son whose loss I have so oft lamented, and let me hope, in you, he will find a second father. Yes, my Reginald," she continued, "no longer Leonard, the fruit of a peasant's loins; know thou art the offspring of Arthur Fitzallan, and rightful heir to all his wide domain, usurped by the villain whom heaven, to do a double justice, doomed to fall by thy all-conquering arm! Hereafter thou shalt know the history of thy mother's sufferings: at present receive the embraces of a sister; love and cherish her!"

Reginald Fitzallan (so we shall henceforth call him) could hardly persuade himself but he was in a dream: to find a parent, and a sister, so worthy of his tenderness, almost annihilated his senses with excess of joy: the titles, and estates, he so unexpectedly possessed, he considered not; save, that it enabled him to place his lovely Emma in a sphere, which nature, lavish in her endowments, formed her to adorn.

On the subsequent day, the Baroness requested to see her son, in her own chamber, where she, according to her promise, recounted the story of her life in the following terms.

CHAPTER VIII

There is a kind of character in thy life,
That, to the observer doth thy history
Fully unfold: thyself and thy belongings
Are not thine own so proper, as to waste
Thyself upon thy virtues, they on thee.
Heaven doth with us as we with torches do,
Nor light them for themselves: for if our virtues
Did not go forth of us, 'twere all alike
As if we had them not. Spirits are not finely touch'd,
But to fine issues: nor nature never lends
The smallest scruple of her excellence
But, like a thrifty goddess, she determines
Herself the glory of a creditor,
Both thanks and use.

SHAKESPEARE.

"SIR Bertram was a Knight renowned alike for courtesy and valour; while yet a youth, he had distinguished himself against the sons of Gallia, and acquired immortal fame: that indeed was all the advantage he derived, though in the service of his country he had spilt his blood, and, for her welfare, devoted the estates of his progenitors; which were so much decreased, as to be insufficient to support the dignity of his family."

"In this exigence he craved the advice of Harold Fitzallan, thy grand-sire, who was his most intimate companion; similarity of manners, and mutual worth, had linked them in the bonds of friendship: up the steep hill, or down the craggy rock, they drove the foaming boar still side by side: in the heat of battle, the shield of Sir Bertram yielded more succour to Harold than himself, while that brave Baron's sword was ever wielded in the defence of his comrade."

"Fitzallan, on being counselled, conjured the Knight to prop his declining fortunes by an advantageous marriage: this, indeed, was the only step he could take, and he resolved to adopt it. The widow of a noble, lately deceased, possessed of immense riches, had long shewn him a marked partiality, of which he now availed himself; he therefore prefered his suit, and met with greater encouragement than his most sanguine wishes had dared to hope: suffice it to say, they were united, and Sir Bertram, though it is not probable he should adore a woman, whose years were ill adapted for the wife of so young a man, behaved to her with tenderness and respect. I am the sole fruit of their nuptials, and bear the name of my mother— Bertha."

"Scarce had I entered on this sea of trouble, when a rumour prevailed, that the Christians again designed to carry their arms into the Holy Land. The thought was transport to my sire, who, fondly hoping he should be enabled to plant the blessed cross upon the walls of Jerusalem, determined to embark in search of victories, which even the illustrious Cœur de Lion had not been able to accomplish."

"He imparted this design to his friend; at the same time urging him to serve under the consecrated banner of our Redeemer. Harold, however, had lately given, not only his hand, but his heart, to a young lady of birth; nor could all the entreaties of Sir Bertram, prevail on him to leave her unprotected."

"Since," said my father, "you will not accompany me, to your charge I confide a treasure, more precious than the treasures of distant India; my infant child: should the fortune of war deprive me of existence, my blood will freely flow, and I shall resign my breath without a sigh, from a conviction of her safety: be a parent to her, so shall my spirit, from its starry mansion, look down, and pour its blessings on your head."

"No more of this;" quoth Fitzallan, "you may live long, and happy: may thy vigorous arm dart through the embattled ranks of Infidels, like heaven's thunder, dealing destruction to the foes of Christ."

"The time for his departure now arrived, and, having taken an affectionate farewell of his consort, and strained me to his breast, he tore himself away."

"My mother, whose heart was fixed upon her Lord, secluded herself from all company, save Fitzallan, and his lady, with whom she fondly anticipated the hour when Sir Bertram should bless her sight. Alas! vain hope! never again was he permitted to view his native land; his bones were left in Palestine, the sepulchre of thousands of his countrymen!"

"Three dreary winters had scarce elapsed from the time of his departure, 'ere the melancholy news of his death was received: he had fallen covered with the wounds of honour, and surrounded by the sabres of Saracens, on whom he discharged his fury; till, overpowered, he yielded his mortal part to earth; his soul to God!"

"His mournful widow, from the time she heard the fatal news, never felt happiness: her friends, in vain, strove to administer the balsam of comfort: the seal of sorrow was stamped upon her form; and, after a tedious painful interval, she followed her Lord."

"This account I had from your grandsire, who would often gaze upon the lineaments of my face, and vow I was the image of his departed friend. I was too young at the time to feel the loss of those so near to me; and the tender assiduities I received, from the noble guardians to whom I was intrusted, prevented my ever experiencing the lack of parents."

"At the castle of Fitzallan, I met your father, their only son; being about my own age, our youthful amusements were the same, and childish partiality ripened, with our years, into mature affection: Harold beheld this, sanctioned our mutual passion, and we were married."

"Death, the destroyer of all human things, deprived us, shortly after, of those much loved parents, and they went from earth, to meet eternal happiness above."

"Our sorrow was excessive; but time, the universal antidote of grief, poured consolation into our bleeding wounds, and
a pleasing regret alone remained: as the rude mariner eyes land,
while the majestic bark, cutting the green waters that lave its
side, diminishes, and, at length, excludes it from his sight."

"A tender infant, my beloved Julia, was a blessing to us, and
heaven promised another, which it gave in you. We now
thought ourselves supremely happy, nor had we a single wish
ungratified."

"Alas! how insubstantial are all human joys: in the sun-
shine of felicity man may bask awhile, but suddenly his prospect is intercepted by an invidious cloud, that leaves him
wrapped in darkness and dismay."

"You may well judge what I mean; the death of thy father;
let me then skim swiftly over a period that, even now, strikes
me with horror."

"When the villain Edmund conveyed me to my prison, in
the *Black Tower*, Providence inspired me with a thought to
save my offspring; I tied a scarf round the body of thee,
Reginald; and, having fastened a portrait of thy murdered sire
about thy neck, dropped thee from the window; having first
scratched upon the back of the picture the following inscription."

"Whoever may find this infant, be careful of him; convey
him far from hence; in his bosom there is a purse, which will
sufficiently reward them: and oh! as they hope for everlasting
mercy, let them not disregard this entreaty."

"Scarcely had I put my plan in execution, 'ere the ruffian,
who was stationed at my door, entered the room, to add some
fuel to the fire. The drowning grasp at weeds to save themselves, and I flattered myself I descried a sensibility in his looks,
that but ill accorded with his occupation, and of which I hoped
to avail myself. I therefore fell upon my knees, and, with all
the energy my feeble strength could summon, implored com-

passion; compassion for one, who had never injured him, even in thought."

"He listened with attention to me, and the drop of pity rolled down his sable beard; yes, inured as he had been to deeds of guilt, my entreaty moved him even to woman's weakness."

"Rise, lady," said he, "pardon what is passed, and if a life, henceforth devoted to your service, can aught atone for the wrongs I have done you, it shall be laid down at your command."

"I thanked him for his proffered service, and anxiously desired he would inform me whether I was indeed a widow? He shook his head, and was silent; but the expression in his countenance spoke more forcibly than any words he could have uttered. Bitterly did I regret the loss of my husband; and, had not my solicitude for the dear pledges left behind restrained my fleeting soul, I should have followed him."

"On returning reason, I flew to the window; but what was my distraction, when I drew the scarf up, to find you, my child, were gone? I feared you had fallen into the hands of Edmund, from whom no mercy was to be expected. Again, hope's delusive shadow fleeted past me, and said you were in safety: my mind was torn by different passions, and fluctuated like the famous Euripus."

"Forgive me, madam," quoth my keeper, "that I interrupt your grief; but, if you take not advantage of the time, an hour may deprive me of the ability to serve you."

"This aroused me, and, taking my beloved daughter in my arms, we issued forth: I having first muffled myself in a soldier's cloak, with which my conductor provided me; and Edmund having fortunately given him his ring, that so he might use his power during the night, we left the castle without opposition, and hurried to the spot whereon I had dropped you, but the place was void."

148

"We then set forth, fast as my frame would suffer me, keeping our course as near the ocean as possible; and on the following morn descried a boat, which was on the point of leaving land for a vessel that lay at about a league distance. My companion inquired of the seamen whither they were bound; they made answer, to the Isle of Wight. All parts of the globe were alike to me, provided I could bear my Julia from the reach of her unnatural cousin; I therefore put myself on board, and departed from my native country: that country where, but a short day before, I thought myself the happiest of mortals; where pleasure waited my command, and where my vassals blessed me whenever I met their sight. Now an exile, driven by the hand of villany from home, and indebted for liberty, nay, possibly life, to the murder of my husband."

"For a moment I doubted the justice of Providence, in thus permitting guilt to lord it over virtue; but soon, very soon, was I convinced of my error."

"A violent gale of wind arose, and, during the hurricane, the captain, with much feeling, entered the cabin, and informed me the surge had broken over the vessel, and swept my servant (so he judged the man who accompanied me to be) from off the deck. This brought conviction to my heart, and I implored the pardon of heaven for my unfounded suggestion."

"The storm increased, and seemed to promise a speedy period to my woes, which I should joyfully have embraced, had it not been for the sweet infant who reconciled me to life. At length, however, the wind died away; the rude blustering of the waves abated, and enabled us to gain our port; where I encountered a person, whose appearance bespoke him noble; he offered his hand to assist me in landing, and begged permission to escort me to whatever part of the island I might be destined."

"I hesitated, stammered, and hardly could refrain from swooning at the question: which he observing, forbore to repeat, and requested I would honour his mansion, for a short time, with my presence. His ingenuous manner banished all distrust, and, I consenting, we arrived at this castle, where an elegant collation was provided."

"During our repast, I observed my host's eyes were rivetted upon me; a melancholy langour overclouded his face, which nature seemed to have taken particular pains in forming. I related my story, and, in return, he favoured me with his, which drew numberless tears from me: my sighs were echoed by his own, and we seemed happy in the company of each other."

"The mind is softened when oppressed, and loves to banquet upon wretchedness: far from seeking jocund converse, it covets the society of those, who, like themselves, groan under anguish; and the pearly drop of mutual pity, is more endearing than the laugh of those untainted with affliction."

"I remained at the castle, and, from the respectful assiduities which were paid me, felt a sincere friendship for my protector; who I found entertained a more tender passion for me, 'though he disclosed it not till the time of my mourning was elapsed; he then conjured me to be his, vowing he would prove a father to my child; who, he said, should never, if in his power to prevent it, know sorrow but by name. I refused his suit, but still he persevered, and, at length, prevailed: Need I say more? I gave my hand *to Hildebrand.*"

"To Hildebrand?" cried Reginald.

"To Hildebrand, my son," quoth Bertha, "for that is the true name of the supposed Montmorenci. His tale, which you shall know hereafter, will convince you he had reason to renounce the former; and teach you, as it did me, that there are no sufferings, how great soever we may imagine them, but others labour under woes as bitter."

CHAPTER IX

You see me here, you gods, a poor old man,
as full of grief as age; wretched in both.

This world I do renounce: and in your sights
shake patiently my great affliction off.

SHAKESPEARE.

REGINALD'S amazement was excessive; it recalled to his mind
the unhappy mortal he had seen upon the Pyrenean hills,
repenting the murder of which he supposed himself guilty;
while his son is compelled to assume a false title, to avoid the
stigma thrown on his family by his parent's rashness.

"What, my dear son, excites thy surprise?" cried Bertha.

"Prepare thyself for wonder," he replied, "for know that the
father of thy Hildebrand yet lives!"

"Lives!" exclaimed she.

"Certain he did, not many months ago: these eyes beheld
him then, bending beneath the double load of age and misery:
with many a drop of sorrow was his recital watered, and the
fate of his Walter lay so heavy on his conscience, I fear his
brain is much deranged. But let us hasten to my worthy host,
and pour the tidings in his ear; it may not be too late, even now,
to bring the old man comfort; the sight of his son will reanimate
his blood, and make him young again."

They hastened to find Hildebrand, Montmorenci no more,
and imparted to him all that Fitzallan knew concerning his
wretched parent: and he determined, on the morrow, to quit
the Isle, in quest of the recluse, Reginald having undertaken to
convey him to the place where he had held his converse with
him. By early dawn, therefore, they departed, and, with an
auspicious wind, soon reached ———, where they landed, and
pursued their route towards the Pyrenees, whose summits are

151

covered with eternal snow, while innumerable flocks, bleached by heaven's fresh blowing breezes, and scarce less white than the drift that overtops them, feed and wanton on their craggy sides.

At length they gained the dwelling of the shepherd, who had before afforded entertainment to Fitzallan, and where they made immediate inquiry after the Man of the Mountain, as he was termed.

"Ah Signore," replied the rustic, "he has not been seen for many a day, and it is imagined he must be dead."

The joy which had shone in Walter's countenance, from the time his young friend disclosed his knowledge of Hildebrand's existence, now gave way to the lowering tints of melancholy. Reginald endeavoured to inspire him with hope, and promised to accompany him over the adjacent mountains.

They searched for two days, but without effect: on the third, the groans of one in jeopardy passed upon the bosom of the air, and attracted their notice. They stopped, and perceived the sounds to issue from a gaping cave, whose sides were overgrown with moss.

"What may this mean?" quoth Walter.

"No matter," returned Fitzallan, "we will enter, and, if in our power, relieve the person that may be therein."

They did so, and, in one corner, beheld a man stretched on a bed, formed of leaves, and rushes. Reginald approached, and discovered it was the object of their search. He waved his hand for his companion to withdraw, then addressed the unhappy being who laid before him.

The sound of his voice awoke the old man, whose cares had found a temporary relief in the arms of Somnus.

"Surely," he said, "I have heard those sounds before! Ah! I recollect; thou art the youth whose friendly converse strove to lull my woes, and which has been the only comfort I have received during a long sojourn on these mountains. Thank

152

heaven! I am near my destined goal, and shall shortly be released from all the miseries that attend this mortal state."

"Not so; many joyful days are, I hope, in store; I come to bring you comfort: your son, your Walter lives; and lives to bless thy aged arms."

Hildebrand looked at him, his eyes sparkling with rage.

"Savage!" he exclaimed, "Cannot the busy world yield scope for merriment and derision, but you must seek, in this secluded spot, a wretch, whose span of life is almost measured? Can humanity be so depraved as to find pleasure in harrowing up the feelings of a poor infirm old man, who is about to render his account to an all-righteous judge that he has dared offend?"

Walter could brook no more, but rushed into the cave, and throwing himself upon the earth beside his parent, cried, *"My father look up, and be of comfort!"*

Hildebrand recoiled with horror!

"Is it possible," he said, "much injured shade, that thou art sent to wring my heart? Alas! there was no cause for this: save me, oh! save me from the horrid spectre!"

His exhausted strength here sunk under the oppression of his fears, and he found a respite in the clasp of insensibility, from which their utmost endeavours were exerted to restore him; when again he began in the same incoherent stile as before, nor was it but with infinite difficulty they could persuade him his offspring lived. At length they poured conviction in his ear, and he returned thanks to Providence, who had thus eased his mangled conscience.

"And now, my Walter," quoth he, "although I dread to ask, tell me, I beseech thee, free of all reserve, does thy mother, my much wronged Eleanor, exist?"

His son answered in the negative, and further informed him, grief for his loss had ended her.

"Is it even so?" cried Hildebrand, "Then I am still a murderer!"

"Think not so hardly, sir," said Reginald, "she fell not by your hand."

"Not by my sword, I grant," returned Hildebrand, "but with as sure a weapon; sorrow, that biting falchion, whose inveterate blade pierces the heart, and bids defiance to the skill of surgery, slew her. Look down, oh martyred saint! from thy celestial throne, and, as my fleeting spirit leaves my clay-cold body, bear it to heaven, and sue for its salvation!"

His voice faltered as he spoke, and the pallid hue, that overspread his features, announced his speedy dissolution.

Walter turned to Owen, "Fly," said he, "for assistance!"

"'Tis all in vain!" quoth the enfeebled dying penitent, "thrice hath the sun gone his revolving course around the globe, since these parched lips have tasted aliment. Take my blessing, and, if the last injunction of an expiring parent hath any influence, bestow thy care upon the future welfare of this good young man. Convey my body to the monastery of St. Antony, to which the peasants will conduct you; in privacy let it be interred, nor over it place any gaudy monument, or superfluous inscription: let the world, if possible, be ignorant where the ashes of such a monster rest, lest they should tear them from their humid bed, and scatter them in air! Farewell, for ever!"

So saying, without a sigh, he resigned his soul, as though it had only tarried for the sad consolation of seeing his offspring, 'ere it departed "for that bourn, from which no traveller returns!"

"And is this all," cried Walter, after a pause, "that remains of thee my father? Where is the fire that was wont to glisten in thine eye, as thou recountedest to me the battles of thy youth? Where the endearing smile that played upon thy favours, as thou diffusedest into my breast the precepts of compassion and religion? Known to the world by name alone! Had none benevolence to prevent the ruthless fang of hunger preying on thee? Alas! while my board was crowned with viands, and the poor suppliant at my portal ever met refreshment, the author of my being, on a bleak hill was pining, devoid of common comfort!"

Reginald, with much entreaty, prevailed upon his friend to quit the cavern, and return to the shepherd's hut; the former with Owen, though much against the 'Squire's inclination, bearing the body of the unfortunate recluse, which, on the ensuing evening, was committed to its mother earth, without pomp or ostentation. The tear of commiseration bedewed his grave, and, after a series of calamities, he rested at last in peace!—

Returning from the monastery to the Abbot, of whom the now Lord Hildebrand had made a gorgeous present; "I have been reflecting," said he, "on the tottering foundation, and instability of human felicity: my father's fate has brought to mind a thousand ideas that never before occurred, and convinced me man cannot make too good an use of life's short journey. In death the peasant, and the prince, meet upon equal terms. Why, then, should they, whom the caprice of the blind goddess have exalted, assume an arrogance, and lord it over their inferiors, when they alike become the food of reptiles?"

Fitzallan sought to eradicate these gloomy thoughts, and to arouze his drooping spirits, by anticipating the moment when they again should see the Isle of Wight. Passing the spot where himself, and Edgar, had first encountered Julia, "Prythee inform me," said Reginald, "is not the castle of the Count Saint Julian near?"

"It is," replied Hildebrand.

"'Tis well!" exclaimed Fitzallan, "we will be his guests, and return the thanks we owe him, for his courteous conduct towards my unprotected sister, while at his mansion. His son, too, shall render me a dear account, or I will tear it from his very heart."

Owen overheard this, and, clapping the spur somewhat roughly against the side of his courser, rode up to his master.

"My Lord," said he, "I hope you will pardon what I am about to say; but, believe me, you had better proceed on your journey homeward, than go out of your road to this same Count: we have had fighting enough already: remember, my good sir, the pitcher that goes too often to the well, is likely to get crack'd at last: and, above all, think of the immense length of their toledos here. Why, *By the valour of my Ancestors!* they would think no more of spitting your Lordship with one, than if you were an orchard rabbit."

"Peace, fool!" returned his master, "nor vex me with thy idle fears."

"Nay, my Lord," cried Owen, "my fears are of too active a nature, to suffer their owner to remain idle. I shall say no more; but, when it is too late, you will confess Owen was your best counsellor."

On the subsequent evening, by sun-set, they gained the castle of Saint Julian: it was a venerable edifice, situated at the foot of an high hill, upon whose side a thick grove reared its lofty crest; which, aided by the present twilight, threw a solemn gloom upon the pile beneath. Silence prevailed unbroken, save by the roaring of a water-fall that rushed impetuously down the mountains steep, and by the croaking of ill-favoured birds, who winged their dusky flight towards their leafy abode.

Approaching, they descried, upon the battlements, a sable standard, which sullenly waved in the hollow gale, and gave an additional gloom to the scene. The sight went to the heart of Owen. "Good heaven!" he involuntarily exclaimed, "protect me, and send me safe out of this cursed place. Oh! a plague on knight-errantry! say I."

"Silence," cried Fitzallan, his eyes rivetted upon the banner, "and strike upon the gate."

156

The woful 'Squire obeyed, though very reluctantly, and raising the massy knocker, it fell with such a crash upon the portal, that the neighbouring hills re-echoed with the sound, and the affrighted Owen hastened to the spot where his companions tarried.

The gate was opened by an aged man, who demanded their business, and they replied, "their wish was to see the Count Saint Julian."

"Enter," said the porter: they did so, and were led into a spacious hall, where the person, who admitted, now left them, but returned in a few minutes, saying, "his Lord was ready to receive them." They were then conducted into an apartment, where they found Saint Julian and his lady.

"To what am I indebted for this visit," quoth the former, rising from his seat, "from cavaliers of whom I have not the slightest knowledge?"

"Can you," answered Walter, "have forgotten Montmorenci, (which was the only name the Count knew him by) at whose castle you met with hospitality; and, in return for which, you would fain have compelled his daughter to receive the hand of a man who was disagreeable to her?"

"Is it possible you are Montmorenci?" cried Julian, "Forgive me, thou best of men, for not immediately recognising one, to whom I am so much beholden: but my eyes are filmed with age; and tears, my dear friend, tears have added to their dimness."

"We expected not your courtesy:" exclaimed Fitzallan, with his accustomed impetuosity; "we demand not hospitality, but revenge. Where is your son, the persecutor of my sister? Well may you start, for know the brother of the injured Julia stands before you. Come, conduct me to him; for, by heaven, and by my hopes of happiness, I swear, revenge shall sate my anger!"

The Count attempted to reply, but bitter sighs, and sobs of anguish, forbade his tongue its office. At length; "Since, then, it must be so," he said, "follow me, and I will lead you to him whose blood you seem to thirst for."

He then took a taper, and ascended a large flight of stairs, at the top of which appeared a door: this he opened, and they entered a large vaulted room, hung with black. Reginald, and Hildebrand, recoiled with horror; but, recovering, they followed their host to a bier in the centre of the room, whereon stood a coffin.

Julian approached it, and, removing the lid, cried, "There is the man you seek."

Fitzallan started: his rage evaporated, and gave way to compassion. To wound the feelings of any being, was what his nature shrunk from, and he inwardly accused himself for causing the grief, he but too plainly observed pictured in the countenance of his host.

"There, there lies the victim of ill governed passion! my poor, ill fated, boy! (continued the unhappy parent, pressing the clay-cold lips of the deceased) we shall meet again never to part more!"

He stood for some minutes fixed, as a statue, and leaning over the bier, until a flood of tears, gushing to his relief, somewhat eased the burthen on his heart; and he moved towards the door, desiring his guests to follow him.

He then returned to the room they had first quitted; and, on his entrance, he requested them to take up their abode, for one night, at the castle: which kindly offer they gladly embraced. Supper was now produced; soon after which the Countess took her leave, and withdrew for the night.

"I am afraid," quoth Julian, not chusing to enter on the subject before his consort, "I am afraid I play the host but ill; yet, I can only say, my heart bids you welcome. The mist of sorrow floats around my head, as the clouds envelop the mountains' top, and forbid the sun-shine of joy to irradiate my aged front. Alas! had my beloved son gone in nature's course, I could have borne my lot with resignation: but to see the pride of my autumnal years lopped from the stem of life, by an assassin's arm, is sure too much to bear!—Your looks bespeak curiosity, and shall be satisfied: I will reveal to you the manner of his unnatural death."

"Though I will frankly own," replied Hildebrand, "it is a subject I wish to be acquainted with; yet would I rather remain eternally in ignorance, than have my inquisitiveness satisfied, by arousing disagreeable reflections in your breast, my Lord."

"That were impossible," cried Julian, "for my grief has never decreased. Wakeing, the recollection of my darling son employs my thoughts: and, when care-worn, I sink, for a short period, into the arms of slumber; the mangled image of my Julian hovers around my pillow, and calls me from my transitory death, to life and misery!"

CHAPTER X

If thou didst but consent
To this most cruel act, do but despair,
And if thou want'st a cord, the smallest thread
That ever spider twisted from her womb,
Will strangle thee; a rush will be a beam,
To hang thee on.——

SHAKESPEARE.

"THE agonies I encounter," continued the Count Saint Julian, "are partly drawn upon myself: to a fond weak indulgence of my boy's foibles, do I ascribe them: may they prove a lesson to future parents to avoid my failing!—Misunderstand me not, by supposing a rigid hand the best to rear your offspring: rigour, as the frost of spring, nips the young plant in the very bud; while too much fondness, like a fierce flame, destroys them. A proper tenderness, seasoned by reason, expands their youthful minds, as the mild rays of Phœbus enrich the soil of nature; and, when they reach the age of reason, they bless you for your care of them."

"Some thirty years ago, I led to the altar Æmelia, daughter and sole heiress to the Marquis Marinelli: a woman cast in nature's choicest mould, and whose personal accomplishments were only to be excelled by the graces which adorned her mind. The only allay to our happiness was, that heaven did not bless us, as we fondly thought, with a progeny. Alas! had the womb of my wife been barren, as the scorching sands of Africa, we had still, perhaps, been happy."

"When every hope was vanished, my Amelia, to my inexpressible satisfaction, confessed herself pregnant. I listened to the declaration, though I could scarcely credit it; but when, after so long an interval, she gave to my arms a son, my joy almost intoxicated me, and, for a while, I forgot to whom I was indebted for the treasure I possessed."

160

"Jachimo, so was the infant christened, increased with his years in beauty; though, from his very cradle, as I may say, his disposition was tinctured by an headstrong impetuosity, that could ill brook restraint; and which, upon every occasion, burst forth. Even among his play-mates, while a boy, there was a superiority in his manner, that set him above the rest, and in all cases of disputes, the arbitration was left to him: but if, on either side, they murmured at the decision of their judge, they were sure to meet with a severe chastisement from him."

"Blinded by affection, I foresaw not the ill consequences attending such a temper; indeed, I considered it merely as the effusion of a noble spirit, impatient of dishonour, and which, I hoped, at a proper time, would be restrained by reason. Alas! vain hope! as he advanced in life, his passions, far from abating, became more fierce, and, like the irruptions of Vesuvius, swept all before them."

"Continual were the complaints preferred against him by my vassals; fathers, whose heads were silvered o'er with age, demanding vengeance for the dishonor of their daughters; others complaining of the barbarous treatment inflicted by Jachimo, on any of the swains who had the temerity to oppose his unjust measures."

"Wearied by these reiterated accusations, I ventured to remonstrate with him on the atrocity of his conduct; conjuring him, as he valued mine, and his mother's happiness, to with-hold from his vile courses; nor endeavour to injure the peace of the poor creatures, my tenants, whose every comfort was center'd in their family."

"Unused to be rebuked, he heard me with a mixture of indignation and contempt; his youthful blood rushed up into his face, and he bit his nether lip with madness."

"Is the noble Count Saint Julian," he cried, "become the champion of a set of wretches, whose very lives depend upon his will? And dare they murmur or complain of his offspring's conduct? What were they created for? To labour and be mute.

I am not singular in my treatment of the slaves. Do not the neighbouring nobles bow their vassals necks to the earth, and treat them as they do their mules and horses?"

"Feeble argument!" replied I, "Is the bad example of another an excuse for acting wrongfully? Or do you suppose these slaves, as you are pleased to term them, feel not the summer's heat and winter's snow, as we do? Why treat them like our beasts of burthen then? They are poor, 'tis true, but they are men; and we offend the Deity, when we degrade a being who bears his heavenly image!"

"Excellent!" quoth Jachimo, striving to smother the rage that I perceived was kindling in his bosom; "had you embraced an holy life, a crosier, long 'ere this, had graced your hand. You have every requisite, believe me: a demure face, an *assumed* sanctity, and an oily tongue, have oft procured a mitre: little more is necessary, and those you have."

"Hold, impious wretch!" I cried, "nor turn to ridicule religion's sacred precepts!—When on the bed of sickness thou art laid, never to rise again, deserted by the friends of thy gay hours, and no companion but thy own reflection, how wilt thou dare to lift thine eyes to heaven, or ask for mercy from that fount thou hast dared to violate with impiety."

"By my soul! this is too much!" exclaimed Jachimo, "rated like a peasant, and all for these vile dunghills! but, if I am the villain they proclaim me, let them look to find me worse, henceforward, than I have yet been. Like the subtle snake, I'll lurk beneath the grass, and, with lynx-eyes, watch every opportunity to sting, and annoy them."

"Monster!" I returned, "full well I know thy sanguinary nature. Like the fell wolf among the bleating flock, thou dealest destruction on my unhappy tenants, because, vile coward! thou thinkest they dare not to oppose thee. But listen to me, wretch! and mark me well; since you indulge the savage disposition of the beast I have mentioned, look to find, in me, an emblem of the animal that guards the herd; and, by my hopes of everlasting happiness, severely will I worry thee!—All ties of nature shall be destroyed between us: thou hast told me my full power; *on my will hangs the existence of my dependents;* I knew it well, and also know thee to be one of them; so take good heed, lest I exert that power to its utmost limit."

"'Tis well," cried he, half choked with choler, "fear not that I shall tarry for you to put your boasted threats in execution. To-morrow, by dawn of day, I quit this hated mansion, never to see it more."

"So saying, he departed the room."

"On hearing this, my anger, like a hasty spark, expired; paternal affection resumed its seat in my breast, and I resolved to exert all my influence in endeavours to prevent his quitting the castle."

"Being summoned to dinner, he entered the apartment, and seated himself, without noticing his mother, or myself."

"Pride, and affection, struggled hard within me; I wished to have continued sullen as himself; but the latter prevailed, and I broke silence."

"Are you determined to quit us, Jachimo?" quoth I.

"Irrevocably," he replied, knitting his brow.

"Come, come," said I, "let me hope you will think otherwise 'ere the morning. We were both warm, perhaps wrong, in our dispute to-day; but it is ended, and let us exchange mutual forgiveness."

"Forgiveness!" answered he, sullenly, "What forgiveness am I to crave of thee? Should a midnight assassin, unprovoked, plunge his stiletto into thee, would'st thou, in reason, supplicate pardon from the vile aggressor? No. Why then am I to crave it from thy hand, who hast insulted and degraded me?"

"Here his mother rebuked him, for his want of duty towards his father; telling him such a headstrong vicious spirit should be kept chained, like a beast of prey."

"Damnation!" cried the impetuous boy, "this is too much."

"Then, starting from his seat, he rushed out of the apartment, and retired to his own."

"In the evening, still a slave to paternal love, I sent divers messages to him, commanding, and entreating his presence; but, equally indifferent to my menaces, and supplications, he positively refused to obey me."

"The victim of anxiety on an ungrateful child's account, I scarcely closed my eyelids during the night; and, no sooner did the first tints of morn break through my window, than I arose, and made inquiry after Jachimo. But what was my grief, when I learned he had quitted the castle above an hour!"

"I was almost frantick, and not only dispatched various messengers after him, but offered a large reward to any that should bring me tidings of him: but all my endeavours were ineffectual, and for one long year did he baffle my searches. At the expiration of that time, I, by accident, got information that he was at Paris."

"Transported at the tidings, I indited a letter to him, filled with words of tenderness, soliciting him, if he valued my existence, and hoped for happiness himself, to return to me."

"This billet, as he has since acknowledged, satisfied his pride, and, in a short time, he arrived here. From my window I beheld him enter the court-yard; the sight seemed to renovate my aged limbs, and, with the alacrity of youth, I may say, I hastened down to him. But, alas! my joy was damped: he received not my ardent embraces with the warmth of a son, who had been twelve long months absent from his native home, but seemingly as an homage, that he thought his right."

"Seldom did he remain a night at the castle, which, I own, awoke my curiosity, and I found means to satisfy it, by bribing his servant; who told me his young lord had, while abroad, formed an intimacy with a young lady, of whom he became so passionately fond, as even to consent to her accompanying him home. That he, the servant, had hired a small house in the neighbourhood for her, at which place Jachimo passed the time

164

that he was absent from the castle. He concluded, by entreating I would keep my knowledge of the transaction from his master; as, otherwise, his life might possibly pay for his want of secresy."

"I promised to lay my finger on my lips, and kept my promise, though I was heartily chagrined at his information."

"Soon after my son's return, your daughter, Lady Julia, arrived here, and unfortunately attracted his notice. He declared to me his love for her; told me he had confessed it to herself, but that she had treated him with disdain, and concluded by swearing bitterly, she should never quit the castle till she became his wife."

"With the subsequent circumstances of that affair, you are acquainted: but to describe Jachimo's rage, on discovering her flight, would be as vain as to attempt to quell the boisterous heaving of Neptune's billows. His fury, however, was too violent to continue; and, when he found all hopes of regaining her were fruitless, his passion subsided."

"Now I come to the crisis, that bears the date of all my woe. Some two months back, at a grand festival given by a nobleman in this vicinity, Jachimo danced with a lady, whose charms instantly enslaved his heart; nor did she return his passion with indifference: she loved him tenderly, and, after a short interval, became his bride."

"They resided with me entirely, and the charms of Adelina seemed to sooth his natural ferocious temper: in short, he appeared an altered being. With rapture I observed the change, and hoped he yet would recompense me for the many unhappy hours I had experienced on his account."

"A few days since, he went, accompanied by a select party of friends, on a hunting expedition, from which he never returned with life."

"Adalina, who existed but in his presence, counted the revolving hours, impatient for the one which was to restore her husband to her arms. Alas! she knew not the misery that then awaited her."

"From one of the western windows, we beheld the sun sink beneath the horizon, and his last golden rays burnish the mountain's tops, but no Jachimo appeared: nor, when the midnight bell, in slow and awful sounds, beat the dead hour of twelve, was he arrived. Unable to account for his absence, and perplexed in vague conjectures, we were sitting, in silent anxiety, when a loud knocking arouzed us from the reverie wherein we had fallen; and the porter immediately entered the room with a small vase, which he said had been left by a stranger, who put it in his hands, and instantly disappeared."

"I was unable to account from whence this present came; but, taking the vessel, and opening it, what was my astonishment, to find therein a *human heart*, and a letter, addressed to Adalina! which was couched in the following terms!"

"As the heart of Jachimo was your's while living, it is but just you should retain it after his death: you will, therefore, find your inestimable treasure in the vase which conveys this to you: while his body, mangled with wounds, lies exposed to birds of prey, a dreadful example to perjured lovers! Know, thou fatal enchantress! I had his plighted vows, 'ere he heard thy syren's voice, or saw thy 'witching face. But of that no more: my dagger has drank his blood, and my revenge is satiated.

CONSTANCE."

"Can I paint the scene then ensued?—Impossible!—A mother bewailing the loss of an only child: a wife deprived of reason from the same cause, and myself obliged to administer the comfort I stood in need of. My heart was nearly rent in twain, and, in the height of my despair, I besought the Almighty to recall the life he gave me."

"Having conveyed my consort, and the frantick Adalina, to their respective apartments, which, with much difficulty, I accomplished, I summoned my domesticks, and repaired to the mansion of my son's mistress, for I had learned her name was Constance; and, at the door, found the corpse of my beloved son, divested of habiliment; disfigured with wounds, and begrimed with blood."

"Part of my servants returned with the corpse to the castle; while the others entered the house of this arch devil, and secured herself, and a female confidant: the latter of whom conjured us to take pity on her situation, affirming, she had been inveigled, and that she was ready to make a full confession of the affair."

"Listen not to her," exclaimed Constance, "nor imagine I shall deny the murder of thy son. Far, very far from it; I rejoice in ridding the world of such a villain: a villain formed for my destruction. I know the rigorous sentence of your laws, and dare to brave them: convey me to my prison, and do, with me, e'en what you please."

"I intrusted them to a proper guard; and then, stupified by grief, for I could consider the whole but as a dream, retraced my melancholy steps to the castle, where I found Æmelia and Adalina, in the same situation as when I left them; nor has the latter yet regained her senses. To-morrow is fixed for the execution of Constance; and may her fate prove a lesson to others, to controul their lawless passions!'"

"You, my Lord, I have injured in the person of your fair daughter: for the which I do entreat your pardon. You see misfortune is come upon my house; and, I think your nature too noble to load a falling man."

Hildebrand assured him of his cordial forgiveness, and they all retired.

CHAPTER XI

——Tis true, I am a king:
Honour and glory too have been my aim:
But tho' I dare face death, and all the dangers
Which furious war wears on its bloody front,
Yet could I chuse to fix my fame by peace,
By justice, and by mercy; and to raise
My trophies on the blessings of mankind:
Nor would I buy the empire of the world
With ruin of the people whom I sway,
Or forfeit of my honour.

ROWE.

CROSSING the hall, in the way to his chamber, Reginald met Owen; who, sticking close to his master's doublet, followed him into his chamber; where, on his entrance, he immediately vented a violent groan.

"How now!" said Fitzallan, "What ails thee, man?"

"Nothing, my Lord," replied Owen, "I was only reflecting on the many pleasant adventures we have met with in our time; and this is, of all others, I think, the most delightfully infernal. I suppose you have heard the story of the young Count Saint Julian?"

"I have," quoth Reginald.

"Well, sir, and do not you think it was a mighty harmless humour of Madam Constance, to send the old Lord his son's heart, as though it had been a present of game? *By the valour of my Ancestors!* mine dies away within me at the bare idea! however, to-morrow the young lady will pay for all."

"Even so; and now leave me," said Fitzallan.

"Leave you, sir?" cried Owen, (his master pointed to the door) "Oh! very well, if I must, why, I must. But, my dear good Lord, will you have the goodness to see me to my own room?

168

Nay, do not frown, for the truth is, I do not much like passing the chamber where this Jachimo lies."

"Leave me instantly," exclaimed Reginald, in a peremptory tone of voice.

"Well, I am gone, sir. I think, though," muttered the woful 'Squire, "when these Knight-errants lead a poor fellow into danger, the least they can do is to see him safe out again. *By the valour of my Ancestors!* these frights will be the death of me at last!"

With these words, Owen retired; but had scarce closed the door after him, 'ere Fitzallan heard a violent crash, like to the rattling of chains; and, at the same moment, some one uttered a loud exclamation of terror: on which he seized a taper, and rushed into the gallery; where he descried his 'Squire extended on the floor, groaning most bitterly.

Reginald applied his foot somewhat roughly to his breech, when again Owen vented a piercing scream.

"How now!" cried Fitzallan, "what panic has seized thee?"

His follower, somewhat assured by hearing his Lord's voice, replied, "the devil himself, I believe, for I never heard such a horrid crash in my life. It came from the deceased gentleman's room: I suppose he has been cramped with laying so long in his wooden doublet, and has got up to stretch his limbs."

Reginald approached the apartment of the young Count, and found his servant's alarm had been created by a ponderous suit of armour, which had fallen from the hook, whereon it was suspended, and which the timid 'Squire, in his present state of mind, had converted into a goblin, or some such terrific being.

Fitzallan having severely rebuked him for his want of courage, returned to his chamber; while Owen, fixing a fearful eye on the door of the deceased Jachimo's room, hurried to his own.

The early tints of rosy morn darting refulgent rays through the window of Reginald's apartment, awoke him: he arose, and repaired to the casement, from whence he beheld the pile, destined for the wretched criminals; who, soon after, made their appearance, and received the punishment due to their enormous crimes.

Reginald then descended into the chamber, where he had been received on his first arrival; and where he found the Count Saint Julian, and Lord Hildebrand: and with the latter of whom, after a melancholy repast, and having taken leave of his unhappy host, Fitzallan departed.

They first proposed visiting England, and soliciting the King to put them in possession of the titles and estates of their ancestors; to which Walter assented: they, therefore, embarked, and the white sails were spread for Albion; auspicious breezes wafted the hulk across the oozy deep, and the anchor was at length fixed in Britain's sand.

They then mounted their steeds, and, riding towards London, in their way they paused one night for refreshment. After regaling themselves, they retired to their couches, and Leonard was buried in deep slumber, when a violent knocking at his chamber awoke him. On opening it he discovered Owen, trembling with terror; nor was it till after some time, he became acquainted with the cause of his panic.

As soon as the woful 'Squire recovered his speech; "Ah, sir!" he cried, "I have news that I know will please you; though, *By the valour of my Ancestors!* it has nearly frightened me out of my wits! I went to the crazy room which was appointed me, and thought to have had a comfortable nap; but there is nothing in this world but disappointments, I think; I reckoned without my host, for I was baffled by the rats and mice, who brushed my nose with their tails, and seemed to be dancing Welch jigs; however, I covered myself with my doublet, and was just entering into a delicious snore, when an unusual noise made me start up, and, looking at the corner from whence it proceeded, I saw a man fast asleep. Curiosity made me wish to have a nearer view of my chum's phiz, and, taking my taper, which burned as bright as an old lady's rheumy eye, I crept softly towards him, and saw it was that devil, Stephen."

"Stephen!" exclaimed his Lord.

"As sure as one and one make two."

"Conduct me to the place," quoth Reginald, then flew to the apartment of Hildebrand, whom he awoke, and who accompanied him to the room where the murderer laid.

The villain opened his eyes; but had the dart of death entered his heart, he could not have looked more pallid. Fitzallan, however, tarried not long, but, procuring a proper guard, ordered them to convey him to the castle in Northumberland, and, also, to secure Gregory, the steward.

On reaching the metropolis, they instantly repaired to court.

The traces of time upon the countenance of Hildebrand, forbade the royal Edward's recognising him: not so Fitzallan; him he recollected, and declared the obligations which he owed him.

Reginald bowed, and addressed his Sovereign in these words.

"Royal Sire, in me you behold the man who shed the blood of Edmund Fitzallan; and I hope the rigour of the law will not deem it justice to despoil me of existence, when it is known I slew him in my own defence, and by so doing, revenged the slaughter of my father."

"Sir Leonard," quoth the King, "I would you had never been guilty of the deed: I respect, I admire you, but did our proper heir stand in thy place, his country should acquit him, or condemn, as though he were the lowest subject of my land."

Hildebrand now spoke, "My Liege," he said, "when you shall hear my testimony, and, if necessary, that of several, I trust you will think otherwise. This youth, the reputed offspring of a peasant, is son to the gallant Arthur Fitzallan, whom

171

the late Edmund barbarously murdered, and usurped his title. Heaven, by miracle, preserved this man, and made him the instrument of justice on the assassin of his sire."

Edward started from his throne, and, rushing towards Reginald, embraced him with all the fervour of paternal affection.

"Welcome!" he cried, "welcome to the arms of one, whose chief felicity and honour, was calling thy noble father friend. Did not thy deeds announce thee his descendant, the resemblance were sufficient to stamp conviction: even as thou now appearest, was thy noble father, when, side by side, we fought our country's battles, and dealt our fury on the foes of England!"

At this encomium on his lost parent, a sigh, half suppressed, burst from the bosom of Fitzallan, and was echoed by his compassionate sovereign, who thus continued.

"The titles and estates of thy progenitors, bought by their valour, and sealed with their best blood, I now restore to thee: what further I can serve thee in, let me but know, and task my power to its utmost."

"Royal Sir," said Reginald, "this my companion, now indeed my father, comes to crave his lands; his name is Hildebrand; a fatal accident, for many a year, has banished him from England, and your goodness emboldens me to second his request."

"Thy boon is granted," replied Edward, "oft have I heard his tale, and oft lamented his misfortunes."

The Barons now took their leave, strongly impressed with gratitude, and instantly dispatched Owen to the Isle of Wight with these glad tidings, and, also, with orders to convey the Baroness, her daughter, and Emma, to the castle of Fitzallan; on which commission he departed, swearing, *By the valour of his Ancestors!* he now bade fair to be a great man!

CHAPTER XII

But, O, how alter'd was its sprightlier tone!
When chearfulness, a nymph of healthiest hue,
   Her bow across her shoulder slung,
   Her buskins gemm'd with morning dew,
Blew an inspiring air, that dale and thicket rung,
   The hunter's call to faun and dryad known;
   The oak-crown'd sisters, and their chaste-ey'd queen,
   Satyrs and sylvan boys were seen
   Peeping from forth their alleys green;
Brown exercise rejoic'd to hear,
   And sport leapt up, and seiz'd his beachen spear.
COLLINS.

REGINALD and Hildebrand, loaded with honours by their illustrious Sovereign, now bade farewell to London, and set out for
Northumberland.

On the fourth day, by early dawn, they gained their journey's end. The morn burst with refulgent splendour, and
seemed to hail the arrival of Fitzallan at his paternal mansion.
The north wind shook the palsied branches of the encircling
grove, and made them bow, as though to own their vassallage to
the adjoining pile, whose stupendous turrets reared themselves
above the leafy labyrinth in towering majesty.

In the vale they were met by the dependents of Reginald,
who flocked in crowds to welcome him; the old and infirm,
hobbled out to meet, and to bestow their benediction on him;
while the more youthful part, with every demonstration of joy,
received him. His heart, not hardened by the luxuriance and
levity of a court, expanded at the sight; he glowed with rapture,
and involuntarily exclaimed, "What wealth can yield a sight
like this, or a satisfaction so substantial as the blessings of our
fellow creatures?"

Suddenly recollecting himself, he dropped his eyes upon the ground, while Hildebrand gave him a look of silent approbation.

By this time they had gained the drawbridge, which was instantly let down, and they passed into the hall; on entering which, Reginald felt emotions never before experienced; the recollection of his father's fate burst on his memory, and forced the pearly drop of sad regret adown his face.

His first deed was to administer justice, latterly unknown at the castle; he therefore cited all his vassals, and summoned Stephen, and Gregory the steward, into his presence. Abashed they appeared before him, nor dared they meet the reproachful eye of him they had so much injured.

"Wretched men!" said Fitzallan, "attend unto me! you stand accused, the one of murder, the other of abetting the foul crime. Have you aught to plead against the charge?"

They were silent.

"Let me hope," continued Reginald, "this dumbness proceeds not from an hardened temper, but from a strong conviction of your error. Now, mark me well! you, Stephen, have acted merely as a tool to your late atrocious Lord, and, did not your sin amount to such a pitch, myself would clear you: but you have imbrued your hands in human blood, and an offended Deity demands revenge. Now for thee, ungrateful savage monster! (quoth he to Gregory, fixing his eyes sternly on him) whom nor the laws of duty, or of hospitality could bind; who connived at the assassination of him your nature should have prompted you to protect; nothing can be said in extenuation of thy crime. To the rigour of justice I commit ye both; and oh! if the faintest ember of expiring conscience burns within ye, intreat mercy of your heavenly judge, but expect no more on earth, than ye yourselves have shewn to others!"

They were then borne away, and, in a short time, paid the forfeiture of their guilt.

Fitzallan now repaired to the cottage of Christopher, wherein he found the owner, and his dame.

"Welcome, my Lord," said the former, bowing lowly, "to the estate of thy ancestors; and pardon, I beseech you, our solicitous care, that so long concealed you from the world."

"This idle ceremony may be dispensed with; ye are my parents still," quoth the youth, embracing them both.

The old woman threw her arms around his neck, and sobbing, cried, "I have now lived long enough: the offspring of my departed Lord is righted, and I have no further business upon earth!"

"May you live happy!" returned Reginald, "my future monitors, as you have ever been! and should this sudden smile of fortune cause me to act unworthily, or to oppress the needy, remind me of my own once humble state, and say, *Is this thy return to heaven for its goodness?*"

The interval 'twixt his arrival and that of Emma, he employed in redressing the grievances of those who had been wronged by his predecessor: he also caused the *Black Tower*, in one of which apartments the gory habit had been deposited, to be converted into a monastery, where oraisons were put up for peace to the soul of the ill-timed Arthur: and moreover sent for the unfortunate Carlos, (the captain of the banditti) who he was sure would be happy to embrace any opportunity of quitting his present disgraceful mode of living. He came, and Reginald disclosed his intentions, asking him if his wishes coincided with them.

"I know not," replied the transported Carlos, "how to thank you as I ought. Thou art some ministering angel, sure, sent from the realms above, to pour the balm of consolation into my bleeding wounds. I accept your proffer as the gift of benevolence, and when I so far forget myself, as to treat your bounteous goodness unworthily, may my sufferings, if possible, be redoubled on my head!"

175

Reginald's heart, dilated with rapture, at being enabled to yield consolation to the unfortunate; and Carlos, in the purlieus of his monastery, repented his involuntary crimes, and sought to render himself worthy to appear in that presence, where, let us hope, his penitence had procured forgiveness.

Every countenance now wore a smile of joy, and the peasants turned their eyes in gratitude to him, who had thus restored the offspring of their former worthy Lord.

From Northumberland, Fitzallan dispatched a courier to Edgar De Courci, acquainting him with the favourable turn in his affairs, and inviting him, and his father, to visit his castle, and complete the happiness he now enjoyed.

In the interim, Lady Hildebrand, Julia, and Emma, reached the valley, escorted by Owen, who prided himself upon the punctuality with which he had executed his commission.

"Here, sir," said he to his master, "here are the ladies; you knew your man, when you sent me to convey them there; I have not only protected, but entertained them, with recounting the names of my ancestors; and had it not been for the flood, I could have traced them farther back than I did. Now, my Lord, after having gone through the torments of those below, I wish to be informed whether our mad schemes are over, or if we are again to sally forth?"

"No," replied Reginald, "our days to come shall be spent in ease, nor shall your parents e'er know want; summon them hither, and they shall be provided for."

"By the valour of my ancestors!" exclaimed Owen, "that is just as I would have it. And, after my many valorous atchievements, I will set myself down, like many other great warriors, and enjoy the rest of my days in peace."

Bertha, on entering the castle, felt emotions known only to the feeling; she dropped many a tear to her Arthur's remembrance: the place she had not seen for many years: when last she beheld its rugged walls, she was flying from her persecutor:

now the mother of a son, who promised to be a blessing to her; and, could she have erased the idea of her first Lord's untimely end, she had been happy.

She requested to see the preservers of her offspring: they appeared, and she loaded them with caresses, vowing they should live henceforward at the castle, and be a witness to the happiness of their adopted son.

"Dear lady!" cried old Barbara, "this is too much; to see my young Lord restored to his rights, was all I dared to hope: but to be repaid for my care of him, by the smiles and approbation of his noble mother, is a joy too great for words to describe."

Even the father of Emma was not forgotten; he had an handsome competency settled on him, nor was he ever up-braided for his behaviour towards his innocent child.

At length De Courci, and his son arrived; the former so much abased in his own eyes, for his unworthy treatment of his young friend, he stood before him like a culprit. The generous Reginald, however, soon reconciled him to himself, assuring the Baron, so far from reprehending his past conduct, he admired his lenity, in merely dooming that man to imprisonment, whom he imagined guilty of having attempted the honour of his wife.

The mention of her name touched the string of discord in the heart of De Courci; for, notwithstanding the injuries he had received at Gertrude's hand, he still remembered her unhappy fate with regret; and a tear stole from his eye to her memory: on which Reginald, who observed the grief he had involuntarily occasioned, shifted the subject, and, in a few minutes, De Courci regained his wonted cheerfulness.

Fearful some unforeseen accident might again deprive him of his mistress, Fitzallan solicited the Baroness to join their hands, as heaven had already done their hearts. The mind of that deserving woman was above all mercenary thoughts; Reginald had riches sufficient to satisfy the ravenous grasp of avarice; and had she placed Emma's merit in the scale, against the treasures of the eastern clime, she would have found her son a gainer. She consented, and the same morn that smiled upon their union, saw Edgar, and the fair Julia, linked in Hymen's rosy fetters.

The shepherds of the valley tuned their rustic pipes; and, with their favourite nymphs, hailed the blessed nuptials of their Lord and Lady. "On the light fantastic toe," they tripped over the greensward; while flaggons of ale, the true old English fare, was distributed amongst them, and, like the inhabitants of famed Arcadia, their happiness consisted in each other.

The ceremony over, the Baroness, clasping her hands in gratitude, thus addressed her children:

"Learn from our past sorrows, and our present joys, that retribution is in the hand of heaven alone. At the great day, when, before the Supreme Omnipotent Judge, our deeds are canvassed; then shall bright Virtue, with exalted crest, meet the all-scrutinizing eye of God; while Vice, abashed, shall hide her wrinkled front, and tremble at the just award of Providence!"

FINIS

APPENDIX

List of subscribers from the first edition (1796)[1]

JAMES AICKIN, Esq. Theatre Royal, Drury-Lane, 2 copies
Francis Aickin, Esq. Gower-Street, 2 copies
Thomas Adair, Esq.
Mr. Aldridge
Mr. Armstrong

J. B. Barrett, Esq. Hay-Market
John Bannister, Esq. Theatre Royal, Drury-Lane
—— Barrymore, Esq. Theatre Royal, Drury-Lane
Mrs. Bland, Theatre Royal, Drury-Lane
Charles Bannister, Esq. ditto
William Bownas, Esq.
Bryan Broughton, Esq.
Mrs. Bower
Mr. Birch, Cornhill
Miss Baxendale, Hart-Street, Bloomsbury
Mr. Bailey
Mr. Butler
Robert Bensley, Esq.

Mrs. Crouch, Theatre Royal, Drury-Lane
Mrs. Clarke
Mr. Crawford, Brighton
Thomas Caulfield, Esq. Theatre Royal, Drury-Lane
Mr. Cross
Mr. Chadwick

Miss Drew

---

[1] In the first edition, the list of subscribers occupies eight pages and can be found immediately after the dedication and before the first chapter of the book. I have included it to show the types of readers (i.e. primarily middle class people, both men and women, and a number of actors) who were interested in the novel in 1796.

Mr. Davison
Edward Dawson
James Dodd, Esq. Theatre-Royal, Drury-Lane
Charles Dignum, Esq. ditto
Miss Dietz, Broad-Street
William Davies, Esq. Theatre Royal, Hay-Market

Miss Ellison
Mrs. Edwin, Theatre Royal, York
Mr. Errington
—— Elliot, Esq.

Right Honourable Charles John Carey, Viscount Faulkland
——Fawcett, Esq. Theatre Royal, Covent Garden
Mr. Fosbrook, Theatre Royal, Drury-Lane
Mrs. Farrell
Miss Franklin
L. Foxall, Esq.
Mr. Freake

Mrs. Glover, Upper Fitzroy-Street
Miss Glover, ditto
Mrs. Goodall, Theatre Royal, Drury-Lane
—— Grubb, Esq. Lincoln's-Inn-Fields
Mr. J. Goddard
George Gutherie, Esq. Dundee
Mr. Gregory, Brighton

Rev. Mr. Hodges
Joseph Holman, Esq. Theatre Royal, Covent Garden
Mr. Holman
Mrs. Hotham
Mr. Haynes, Theatre Royal, Covent Garden
Miss Hale, Theatre Royal, Drury-Lane

Mrs. Jordan, Theatre Royal, Drury-Lane
Miss Innes
John Johnstone, Esq. Theatre Royal, Covent Garden
Mr. Johnson, Cambridge-Street

William Jewell, Esq. Theatre Royal, Hay-Market
Mr. Jones, Great Queen-Street

John Philip Kemble, Esq. Theatre Royal, Drury-Lane
Thomas King, Esq. ditto
Michael Kelly, Esq. ditto
Charles Kemble, Esq. ditto

Madam Le Blond
William Lee, Esq. 2 copies
Mr. Lewis

Lieutenant Col. Morris
Miss E. Mauleveror
Mrs. Michell
T. C. Mitchell, Esq, Brighton
David Morris, Esq. Park-Street
John Moody, Esq. Theatre Royal, Drury-Lane

Miss Newman
Miss E. Newman
Henry Nelson, Esq.

Mr. Oliver
Mr. Oliphant

Dr. Petre
Mrs. S. Porter, Welbeck-Street
Stephen Porter, Esq. ditto
Miss Pope, Theatre Royal, Drury-Lane
Mrs. Powell, ditto
John Palmer, Esq. ditto, 2 copies
Robert Palmer, Esq. ditto
Mr. Packer, ditto

Mr. Reading
Mr. Reed

Lady Charles Spencer

Mrs. Siddons, Theatre Royal, Drury-Lane
Signora Storace, ditto
Richard Suett, Esq. ditto
—— Shaw, Esq. ditto
Thomas Sedgwick, Esq. ditto
Samuel Sewell, Esq.
Charles Smart, Esq. Norfolk-Street
Mr. Simms

Mrs. Turner

Mrs. Vernon, Broad-Street
Miss Vernon, ditto
Adj. Joseph Mortimer Vernon, Madras
Lieut. John Vernon, ditto

Miss White
J. Wade, Esq.
Mr. R. Watkins
Mr. Wright
Mr. Wilmot
Mr. Wilde
R. Wilkinson, Esq.
Thomas Wroughton, Esq. Theatre Royal, Drury-Lane
—— Wathen, Esq. ditto
—— Whitfield, Esq. ditto
Mr. Waldron, ditto

Mr. T. Young

APPENDIX

Contemporary review of *The Mystery of the Black Tower*

The Mystery of the Black Tower. A Romance. By John Palmer, Jun. Author of the Haunted Cavern. 12mo. 7s. Lane, 1796.

It appears essential to romance, that the scenes it describes, should either be remote from the times in which we live, or the people with whom we converse. The first of these rules has been obeyed by Mr. Palmer; and he has thrown his scenery back into the reign of Edward the Third, an æra of chivalry and warlike enterprise, perfectly favourable to his design. His conception of the subject is, in other respects, sufficiently just: and by the introduction of a facetious Welch Squire, he has enlivened the solemnity of his graver scenes, with occasional flashes of humour. The romance is certainly executed with ability; and discovers such talents for that species of composition, as may be said to merit the protection of the public.

—— *British Critic*, December 1797, p. 435.

Gothic Classics

NOW AVAILABLE

THE ANIMATED SKELETON, Anonymous
128 pp. March 2005 0-9766048-0-9, $13.95

THE CAVERN OF DEATH, Anonymous (Ed. Allen Grove)
104 pp. July 2005 0-9766048-3-3, $12.95

THE CASTLE OF OLLADA by Francis Lathom
192 pp. March 2005 0-9766048-2-5, $14.95

ITALIAN MYSTERIES by Francis Lathom
400 pp. July 2005 0-9766048-6-8, $16.95

MYSTERY OF THE BLACK TOWER by John Palmer, Jun.
200 pp. August 2005 0-9766048-1-7, $14.95

THE PHANTOM OF THE CASTLE by Richard Sickelmore
128 pp. June 2005 0-9766048-9-2, $13.95

COMING SOON

GASTON DE BLONDEVILLE by Ann Radcliffe (Ed. Frances Chiu)

ANCIENT RECORDS by T. J. Horsley Curties

WHO'S THE MURDERER? by Eleanor Sleath

All titles are available at www.valancourtbooks.com or from
any fine local or online bookseller.

Valancourt Books, P.O. Box 220511, Chicago, Illinois 60622
http://www.valancourtbooks.com   gothic@valancourtbooks.com

Printed in the United Kingdom
by Lightning Source UK Ltd.
134487UK00001B/226/A